Red Smoke

Red Smoke

Veronica Fuxa

ISBN-13: 978-1-4952-8618-6
ISBN-10: 1495286185

First published in the United State of America in 2013.
This edition published in 2014

In Memory of my Grandpa,
Thomas Roberts.

Chapter One

"I'll get you!" I shouted to my little sister. She squealed and ran faster down the street. I struggled to keep up with her. Anne is only 10 years old, yet she can outrun anyone in Amsterdam. She zipped around the corner past Oliver's Grocery. Oliver was closing up his store for the night.

"Hello, Anne and Jenna," he greeted.

"Hello, Oliver," we both yelled. I was gaining on her when two men walked in front of us. They were carrying a long, mahogany table. I hit the brakes and shouted, "Anne, stop!"

Anne kept going at full speed. She took one flying leap over the table and barely made it over. She stumbled a little on her landing, but she made it! She turned around to see the men staring at her in awe. She gave them a smug grin. I dashed around them and hugged her, "Are you ok?"

She smiled at me, "I'm fine. Looks like I won."

"Yes, you won," I chuckled, still catching my breath. "Are you part gazelle?"

We laughed and skipped all the way home, singing songs and dancing like fools. This is what Anne and I did every day after school. We'd race each other all the time. Anne usually won though, but it kept me in good shape. Anne was the star athlete of our school anyway, so I don't feel too bad when I lose.

We arrived at our small apartment complex a little late, only six minutes after curfew. We dashed upstairs, and as soon as we arrived at our door, it swung open.

"There you girls are! I've been worried sick!" Mother cried. I hung my coat and looked down sheepishly. Before our race, I had wanted to treat Anne to some hot chocolate, only to find that the only café that served Jews, The Cream Café, was closed. Many places that serve Jews are closing down. It's hard enough to find a toothbrush or soap these days.

I nudged Anne and said, "Sorry, Mother."

Anne nodded, "We're sorry."

Mother sighed, "You know that it is after curfew. Do you know what will happen if the Gestapo finds you?"

I nodded and looked down at my shoes. My good friend, Greta Kensley, was sent to a death camp for being out after curfew. Her whole family went a few days later because they were Jewish. I nodded, "Yes, we know. It won't happen again."

"It better not. Girls, do you have homework?" she asked.

Anne groaned and got her books out. She really didn't like her new teachers. I didn't like mine either. After our old school, Sentory Public School, banned all Jews, we had to go to King United with other Jewish kids. I hate it there. None of the teachers are nice, and the students are so glum. I haven't made any new friends yet and neither have my sisters.

Emma walked into the room, "The neighbors won't stop yelling! I can't study for any of my tests with them fighting nonstop!"

Mother sighed, "I'll see what I can do. Just study in here with your sisters. Soup is for dinner."

"When will Papa get home?" Anne asked anxiously.

"Soon," Mother answered.

Anne finished her math before me. She is six years younger than me, yet she can do my Algebra. She helps me with that, and I help her with grammar. I'm really good at it. I guess it's a natural talent of mine. I think I get it from Papa. He was a writer at the newspaper, The Amsterdam Weekly.

Emma offered, "I'll check your papers if you'd like."

We immediately hand our papers to her. Anne and I may be smart at some things, but Emma is smart at *everything!* There is not one subject she isn't good at. She's a straight A student. Maybe she'll be someone great someday. We need someone to help us rise from the ashes. Emma is a great leader, and I know she could do something like that.

I couldn't though because I'm too shy. I can't even talk to boys, or make new friends. I could see myself as a writer maybe, or an editor of a magazine. I could travel the world and write about all my adventures. That is my dream job.

After dinner, Emma and I did dishes. She kept going on and on about this boy that she likes. *Groan!* Who is it this week? I think his name is Arnold. I really don't pay attention when she talks about boys. I used to, but then there were so many boys I lost track of who we were talking about. Emma is very pretty, it's no wonder why so many boys like her.

She's strong, beautiful, and smart like my mother, and Anne is the same way. They both look like Mother with their bright, green eyes and black as night hair with porcelain skin, thin body, and very tall stature.

On the other hand, I am very short. I have long, blonde hair and big, blue eyes. My skin is pasty white and I'm not skinny, but I'm not fat. I get all of my characteristics from my grandma. We were so close. She died of pneumonia last winter. I once saw a picture of her when she was my age, and we look exactly alike! It's uncanny!

I heard a bang on the door. Anne ran to go get it. She cried, "Papa!"

Papa came in looking tired. He brightened up when he saw Anne, "Hello, my angel!"

I dashed to hug him. He patted my head. I looked up at him. He has a funny face. His nose is too big, and his eyes are too small. He has big bags under his eyes from lack of sleep and wrinkles from smiling too much. His smile is slightly crooked and that made you want to smile. He laughed, "What are you looking at, small stuff?"

I giggled, "Nothing pretty. Papa, you're late again!"

He sighed and the smile ran away from his face, "I know. Where is your mother? I need to . . . talk to her."

Mother appeared beside me. She smiled and kissed Papa on the cheek. She said, "There you are, Charles. I was worried."

"Mary, we need to talk," Papa said seriously. Mother's smile disappeared, and she walked to the kitchen. He hung his coat up and followed her.

I gazed at his coat. The Star of David is worn out and faded on it. We all have to wear it now. It was hard explaining it to Anne.

"Why do we have to wear this?" she had groaned.

"It is a symbol that represents our religion, and we shall wear it proudly," I had explained. "It shows everyone who we are."

"Does it matter for everyone to know who we are?" she had asked. "Can't we have privacy?"

I had laughed at this. At the time, I thought it was so funny, "Of course we have privacy! Don't you want to be proud of your religion?"

Now, we don't have privacy. We live in dirty, crowded ghettos. Fortunately, we don't have any roommates with us. My friend Joshua has three families living with him. It gets loud at night; people talking and babies crying. Sometimes I hear Anne next to me crying because she can't sleep. I always comfort her until she goes back to sleep. It breaks my heart to see her cry.

Emma rushed into the room and whispered, "Papa said he lost his job! They fired him!"

3

Anne and I were shocked. She whimpered, "You're serious? They fired Papa? Why?"

She started sniffling. I hugged her tightly and brushed her black hair to comfort her. I looked at Emma. She had tears in her eyes. We knew what this meant. We had to get jobs. Mother barely got any money from her cleaning job. Papa is the only real source of income in our family. I am 16 years old, and Emma is 17 years old. We're old enough to work, but are there any jobs for Jewish girls?

I heard Mother sobbing loudly in the kitchen. We crept inside to find her sitting next to Papa. He was rubbing her back and murmuring something in her ear. He looked at us and opened his arms up. Anne ran for the hug, but I hesitated. Emma didn't move, and I wanted to be strong like her. I built a strong wall inside me and stayed put. Mother let out another wail. Emma suddenly rushed to her side, choking on her tears.

I stood alone. Papa looked at me again, his eyes wet with tears. My strong wall crumbled, and I ran to him. I buried my face into his neck. He sighed, "Oh, my girls I'm so sorry. It's my fault!"

Mother sobbed, "No it isn't. They only fired you because you're Jewish! Why would that matter to them? You're an amazing journalist!"

We stayed huddled close together until Papa slowly stood up, "Girls, you should go to bed."

Emma quickly ushered us to our only bathroom. We brushed our teeth and combed our hair before we went to bed. I crawled into bed next to Anne. We shared a bed and a room with Emma. She got her own bed though, since she's the oldest. Mother and Papa sleep in the living room.

Emma wrote in her journal. I need to get one of those. Anne breathed softly next to me. I smoothed out the wrinkles on the lacy nightgown my grandma had given me. It was the last birthday present I had received from her.

Papa came in to kiss us goodnight. He kissed Emma's forehead and whispered something to her. He walked over to me and smiled then touched Anne's forehead softly, "Is she asleep?"

I nodded, "I hope she stays asleep tonight."

He kissed her forehead then whispered to me, "Jenna, there will be tough times ahead. I want you to be strong for me, your mother, and Emma, but most especially Anne. She looks up to you like you do to Emma. Be strong and brave for her."

I nodded and felt a small tear go down my cheek. He wiped it away. I whimpered, "Sorry I . . . I'm just so scared."

He chuckled softly, "What is there to be scared about? You have your family don't you?"

I nodded.

"Well as long as you have us, there is absolutely nothing to fear. Families takes care of each other no matter what."

I smiled, "I love you, Papa."

"I love you, Jenna. Did I tell you your eyes are bluer than the sky?"

I laughed, "And deeper than the ocean? Yes, Papa, a thousand times."

He smiled, "Well make that a thousand and one."

He kissed my forehead and shut the door. I slowly fell asleep.

Chapter Two

"Wake up!" Emma whispered fiercely.

I groaned, "What time is it?"

I felt a pillow smack my face. I sat up abruptly. Emma was packing things into her suitcase. She hissed, "Get up! We need to pack now! Wake up, Anne!"

I shook Anne. She grumbled and pushed me out of bed. I tumbled to the floor. I got up and shook her harder. She opened her eyes and glared at me, "What are you doing?"

"Emma says to get up and pack!" I said in a serious tone.

"Why?" she whined.

I looked over at Emma, "Why?"

Before she could answer, Mother opened our door. Her face was pale and her eyes bloodshot. She twitched nervously, "Are you packed?"

Emma answered quickly, "They just got up, but I got most of their stuff packed."

Mother stuttered, "W-we d-d-don't have m-much t-t-time."

I heard a loud voice come from the living room. It sounded like a soldier. I asked, "Mother, what's going on?"

Mother flinched at a loud bang, "Everything is f-fine. Be r-ready in three minutes."

She shut the door. Anne and I looked at each other and then at Emma. She flew around the room, throwing things in her already full suitcase, "Jenna, help Anne pack. Make sure you put warm clothes in. Don't forget your boots! Pack your toothbrush too."

I put in five dresses, four pairs of tights, my toiletries, my boots, my gloves, my knit hat, and my shoes. I could barely close the case! I helped Anne with her suitcase. Mother came in with a grave look on her face. I noticed a small cut on her forehead.

Emma led us out of our room. I looked around wildly, trying to take everything in. The soldiers were pushing Papa out the door. Mother ran to his side. Emma held Anne's hand. I looked back at our little apartment as we were forced out the door. I felt a strong hand turn my head around and push me forward.

They loaded us into a truck filled with other people. Papa and Mother went in first and next was Emma. I helped Anne inside the truck. I noticed the soldiers didn't even bother with our bags.

"What about our bags?" I asked.

"Move it!" yelled a soldier. He pushed me onto the truck. I hope he didn't see under my gown. I realized that I'm still wearing my nightgown and so were Anne and Emma. I huddled between them. Anne buried her face into my lap, and I held her close. Father held Mother, who was in complete hysterics, and Emma was stone. She was completely emotionless and unmoving. I wish I could be as strong as Emma, but I just couldn't hold my fear in anymore.

I bawled and buried my face into Anne's hair. It smelled so sweet. I wish I could just stay like this. I wish I was back in my bed. I wish this was only an awful nightmare. I pinched myself hard. Wake up! Wake up!

A baby cried in my ear. I heard the mother trying to shush it, making it scream louder. I heard people moaning in pain, saying that we will all die.

Papa touched me, "Girls, listen to me. I need you to be strong and brave. I need you to be strong and brave even when you want to be weak and scared. We may get separated, but I want you to know now that as a family, we will never be separated. In our hearts, we will stay together. Mary, take good care of the girls. I love you, my dear. Emma, take care of your Mother, and be strong for your sisters and me. I love you, my darling. Anne, you are the youngest, but you are just as brave as your older sisters. I love you, my angel."

He pulled my face to his. He looked hard into my eyes, "Jenna, I want you to be strong for Anne. She's your little sister, protect her. I know you think you aren't strong or brave, but I believe in you. Remember that your eyes are bluer than the sky and deeper than the ocean. I love you, my princess!"

I nodded my head because I couldn't speak. An old man snapped at us, "Ladies, don't listen to any of that! We're all going to die. It doesn't matter how strong or brave you are! Your father is a liar!"

Papa said in his calm, soothing voice, "Sir, we aren't going to die."

"Oh, what a lie!" he hissed.

The truck bounced along the road for what seemed like ages. My legs were cramping up. I wanted to stretch out so badly. I couldn't believe Anne was still in a heap in my lap, her legs tucked under her body. Suddenly, the doors opened and soldiers yelled for us to come out. I jumped to the ground and helped my family out of the truck. Papa stayed to help the mother and her child.

We were at a train station. People were being loaded into huge train cars. Orders were shouted in German. Soldiers pushed and shoved people to the trains. It was total chaos.

I looked down at Anne. She trembled in fear at the chaotic scene. I took her hands, "Look at me. Mean people are going to tell you what to do. They're going to beat down on you and tell you you're stupid, useless and ugly. Do as they say, but don't believe their mean words. You are absolutely perfect, Anne. Never forget that I love you and nothing will stop me from protecting you."

"O-ok," she stuttered.

"Move!" shouted a soldier. "Faster!"

I pulled Anne with me. Emma held Mother's hand. Mother looked behind and called, "Charles, hurry!"

Papa jogged to us. A soldier grabbed his shoulder and commanded him in German. Papa pushed him off and continued to us. Two more soldiers tackled him and beat him to the ground. Mother ran to him screaming and shouting. Emma pushed us forward, "We need to get on that train."

Anne protested, "What about Mother and Papa?"

Emma shook her head, "We'll meet up with them on the train. Let's go!"

I looked back at my papa. He told my mother to go, but she wouldn't listen. I've never seen her so angry. Three soldiers were holding her back, yet she still ran for him. She was swearing and biting and screaming. Papa seemed so calm, like he knew what he was doing. He kissed Mother one last time. A soldier grabbed him by his hair and dragged him away.

That was the last time I saw Papa.

Emma pulled me along. I gripped Anne's hand hard. I watched the pandemonium. Wives stripped of their husbands, children separated from their families, soldiers whipping innocent people. Why is this happening to us? What did we do to deserve this?

A slap on my back interrupted my thoughts. A soldier pushed me forward, "On the train. Move it!"

I looked at the train car. It was already packed full of women and children. Shouldn't we get on a different one? One that is less crowded.

Emma was already up on the car and helping Anne. I was so short; I could barely get my foot up! Someone from behind pushed me and I banged my head. I touched my forehead, it was wet with blood. I probably have a nice gash. Emma pulled me into the car. She led us to a corner. She searched the wall, like she was looking for something. I had no clue what she was doing, so I focused on Anne.

Anne shook violently and chattered her teeth. It was very cold outside. I hugged her tightly, trying to keep her warm. I breathed softly and could see my breath. Anne's cold hand touched my neck, and I felt chills run down my spine.

Emma gestured me to the wall. She pointed at a small hole in the wood wall. She whispered, "See that? That will be the only air and light coming into the train. When they shut the door, it will be very dark. We need to cover it, but we can use it to breathe fresh air. Don't let anyone see it."

"Why not?" Anne asked quietly. "Shouldn't we share the air?"

Emma sighed, "Right now we need to keep ourselves alive."

"Papa says we should always share with others," Anne quoted.

"Papa isn't here is he?" snapped Emma. Anne was shocked by Emma's tone and started to cry. Emma sighed and patted her back. "I'm sorry, Anne. I didn't mean to snap like that. I . . ."

Her voice faded away. She looked at me and whispered in my ear, "Block the hole until I come back. I'm going to find Mother."

Emma dodged women and children on her way back to the doors. I sat in front of the hole and made sure it was covered. Anne sat in my lap and cried until she ran out of tears. She started to violently shake and hiccup. I rubbed her back gently. I think she fell asleep.

I observed the other women and children. They were all like me. Human. They didn't have a third arm or eye. They didn't have violet hair or crimson skin. They were normal, like me. Like everyone else. So why are we in a train car being shipped off?

A girl my age carried a little baby in her arms. She looked around desperately searching for someone. The baby cried loudly. She looked down at it, her brow furrowed in thought. She set the baby down on the floor and ran away. My eyes widened. The baby could be squished, but I was too far away to save it. A woman was pushed backward, and she accidently kicked the baby. No one noticed the loud squeal because it was drowned out by the other noises.

Emma rushed to me carrying Mother. Both of them looked awful. Dirt and blood stained Emma's nightgown and mud covered Mother's hair. Her arms were covered in dried blood. Scratches and gashes decorated her face. Emma set her down and sat beside me. She was out of breath, "They beat Papa . . . to death. Mother wouldn't leave. She was . . . was . . . protecting Papa's dead body."

I hope Anne didn't hear that. I had no clue what to tell her when she wakes up. Emma burst into tears and hugged me. I let her cry into my shoulder. Mother shook in front of me. I was afraid to talk to my own Mother! Suddenly, the doors shut and it was pitch black.

Chapter Three

We huddled together in the dark. Anne rested in my lap. Emma sat on my right side, and Mother sat next to Emma. We took turns breathing the fresh air and made sure no one saw us. We had to be very careful since it was so dark. Anyone could easily look at us and see a flash of light.

The moans and cries were deafening. There were at least 20 babies crying. Children cried for food and water. There weren't any restrooms either. The smell of urine and feces stank up the train car. Anne threw up in my lap. She was so embarrassed, she started crying again.

Mother won't talk to us. She stays in the corner and talks to herself, mainly about Papa. Emma and I are worried about her. Emma asks Mother if she wants to talk about Papa, but she never answers.

There is absolutely no wiggle room in the car. Women and children keep stepping on each other. My toes are bleeding from people stepping on them. Children can't run around and stretch out so they become restless and impatient. Women try to sit down, but they can't move far enough to lower themselves to the ground and there's the chance someone will step on you. Luckily, we were crammed into a corner, but we were still stepped on.

The boredom really starts to get to me. All I can do is sit still and breathe. The air in the car is so hot and smelly and the body odor is so foul! We were fortunate to be able to breathe out of the small hole in the wall.

Mother still won't talk, Anne won't keep a conversation for long, and Emma was barely keeping it together. Her face was so tense that it could shatter like china plates at any second.

I wish I had some playing cards. Papa and I played card games all the time. I like playing solitaire by myself. I had tried teaching Anne one time, but she didn't pay attention. But of course, there was not enough room to play cards. There wasn't even enough light to see cards. I just wish there was something to do.

I felt an urge in my bladder. I suddenly had to pee very badly. I whispered that to Emma. She gave me a look that said, "That's not my problem." I made her hold Anne. I tried to relax and just let it all flow out. My body wouldn't let me though. It was confused because I wasn't sitting on a toilet with my underwear down. Instead, I'm sitting in a train car wearing a torn, sheer nightgown.

It seemed like fifteen minutes had passed by, and I haven't gone yet. Emma mumbled, "Think of water, like waterfalls or flowing rivers."

I thought of the river Thames in London. I felt warm urine soak my underwear and nightgown. I felt like crying. I haven't wet my pants since I was five years old. Here I am, 16 years old, peeing in a train car.

You couldn't tell if it was night time in the train car. I could tell it was dark outside by the hole, but most people in here couldn't. Children moaned and cried for sleep. There wasn't enough room for anyone to lie down. I was able to move Anne on my lap. Women by the walls propped their bodies up against it and slept standing. Women in the center of the train just plopped on the ground holding their children in their laps. The rest had to stand or lie on top of someone.

Emma leaned on me and Mother leaned on her shoulder. I cradled Anne in my lap and leaned against the hole in the wall. It was hard to sleep with all the noises, but somehow I managed to drift off.

Days seem to run together. I feel like I've been in this car for months, but it has only been three days . . . I think. I have used the restroom once all over myself. I feel so dirty. My hair has lost its shine, and my ears were full of earwax and dirt.

My stomach won't stop growling. Mother tried to get us to eat lice from our hair. I caught Anne trying to eat one. I immediately flicked it away and scolded her. In her defense, she whined, "But I'm so hungry!"

Mother won't stop talking about Papa. She keeps saying he will come rescue us. Even though he is dead, she talks about him as if he were still alive. Finally Emma lashed out at her, "Mother, Papa is dead. He will never save us!" Mother didn't say anything back.

One day, the car started slowing down. Suddenly, I didn't feel like we were moving at all. The car wasn't jumping or shaking. The door opened and the light blinded us. I heard a rough voice yell, "All the elderly and babies come out."

Emma rushed to the doors. I told Anne to stay put with Mother. I stumbled after Emma. We watched the poor, old women jump out of the car. They landed in a crippled heap. Babies were handed to the soldiers. Mothers hollered and protested as their babies were lined up with the old women.

Some young women just flung themselves out of the car, as if they had nothing to live for, or maybe just to get it over with. One landed on her right leg wrong and I heard an awful snap. I felt myself grab Emma's hand. She squeezed mine tightly.

A woman handed a wailing child to a soldier. He let it slide through his hands to the ground. I heard a sickening *crack*, and the wailing stopped. The mother cried and crumpled to the ground. Women encircled her trying to help her up.

I heard a loud gasp behind me and turned around. Anne stood there, her eyes big as pot bottoms. She looked at me with great pain on her face. Her face was frozen in horror. I hugged her tightly, "Anne, I wish you didn't see that!"

What she said, almost made me collapse to the ground, "It doesn't matter. I believe worse things will happen."

That thought coming from my 10 year old sister, who always smiles and laughs, almost made me want to jump like the others. Her usual mirthful tone was now a cold, stony utter. She sounded just like Mother. I sent her back to Mother with Emma.

I stayed by the doors. I wanted to smell the fresh air before it was replaced by the smell of feces. I checked my gown in the light. The white lace at the bottom was yellow and green from Anne's throw up and my pee. I felt a tear run down my cheek. Suddenly, something wet licked my face. I shouted and turned to my right to see a young woman with wild eyes staring back at me. She begged, "Please, just cry a little more. I've run out of tears and I'm so thirsty."

Of course I bawled. My hot tears streamed down my dirty face. She kept licking my tears. I hope Anne, Emma, and Mother didn't see me. I hope Papa didn't see me.

The doors shut again and darkness surrounded us. I ran away from the woman. I found my way back to my family. I huddled next to Mother, wiping my face.

Even though we couldn't see, we could hear. I'm sure everyone in the car heard the gunshots. The dying wails of babies and old women. My cries blended in with the others.

I woke up in Mother's lap. I sat up stiffly, stretched my arms out, and checked on Anne. She was still asleep. She hasn't been the same since the baby incident. I tried to talk to her and cheer her up, but it doesn't work and it only makes me feel more depressed.

The train car stopped. I shook everyone awake. The doors flew open, and women and children jumped out of the cramped train car. Emma helped Mother up and I pulled Anne up too. Soldiers were shouting outside, but I couldn't understand what they were saying. I whispered in Emma's ear, "Do you understand what they are saying?"

She answered, "No. I know they are speaking German, but they are talking too fast. Papa was teaching it to me, but I don't know very much."

It may be German, but it just sounded like they were shouting angry words around. We stepped off the car. My legs felt weird from crouching down for so long. Anne stumbled to the ground. I pulled her up, "You need to stand up and stretch your legs."

She stood up and stretched. Her back made a loud pop. For the first time in days, Anne giggled, "That felt fantastic!"

Seeing Anne so happy put a smile on my face. I bent backwards and popped my back. It did feel nice. Emma popped hers and sighed, "Much better."

Mother looked at us as if we were strangers. She then looked around with a frightened look on her face. I touched her shoulder and she flinched. I gave her a reassuring smile, "Be brave for Papa, Mother."

She nodded, but I don't think she really heard what I had said. She almost looked like a corpse. I looked at Anne. Her gown hung limply on her. Her hair was a tattered mess and so was Emma's. I felt my caved in stomach, and I could count my ribs! I suddenly felt very nauseated. I don't know how long we were in there, but I was starving.

A blonde soldier approached our group. He barked orders in German. We looked around to see if anyone knew what he was saying. A tall woman translated, "He says we need to undress. We are taking showers."

The blonde soldier nodded. I glanced at Mother as she undressed along with the other women. I looked at Emma. She awkwardly pulled her dress off and pulled down her underwear. She looked over at me and gave me a reassuring smile. She mouthed, "Go help Anne."

I checked Anne. She shook like a leaf. I walked to her, pulled her dress over her head, and shielded her as she pulled off her underwear. She also shielded me when I undressed.

I looked around at the soldiers. I've never undressed in front of men before. The feeling of disgust was almost paralyzing. They were watching us intensely. Some whispered and pointed at us. Some of the soldiers would approach women and harass them. They would poke their chests and make obscene gestures. If they touch Anne, I will hurt them.

I finished undressing and stepped away from Anne. The blonde soldier stared at me for an uncomfortable amount of time. I looked down at myself. I was so skinny, but isn't that what I've always wanted? Now it doesn't looks so good.

I looked over at the other train car. The soldiers opening it were throwing bodies out of it. Dead bodies. A small group of women huddled together. They cried over the bodies. One kept shaking a young girl. She shook her shoulders and screamed for her to wake up. It reminded me of my mother screaming after my Papa. I couldn't watch anymore. Her screams will forever be embedded in my memory.

The blonde soldier escorted our group to the showers. We walked huddled together, trying to shield our naked bodies as best as we could. I saw another group being escorted to another building. The building was in the distance. It looked like a big bunker. I saw smoke rise from three chimneys on top of the building. It wasn't black smoke though; it was red smoke. Someone said it was from human bodies. How can they know that? Why would they be burning bodies?

I wanted to tell the group to run; to join us to the showers. Or are we even going to the showers? I felt my heart race. Will I be helpless to watch my sisters and mother die? I wonder if the people marching to the building knew they were going to die.

We approached the shower building. I paid close attention to the top. I didn't see any chimneys or smoke rising. The blonde soldier noticed me examining the building. He pushed me forward with the rest of the group.

Inside the room, it was dimly lit. There were six shower heads. Twenty people gathered around each one. I heard Emma whisper, "Wash Anne."

I grabbed Anne's hand and led her to one. I couldn't find a bar of soap, so I used my hands to wash the dirt and throw-up from her body. The water was freezing cold, but it felt and tasted wonderful. It was great to have water rolling down my back. It made me think how lucky I was to have hot water back in the apartment.

I looked around for Mother and Emma, but I couldn't see them. I looked for towels to dry ourselves off, but I couldn't find any. A soldier walked in and pointed outside. We shuffled out of the building. It was morning still and it was very cold. I shivered as we ran back to the train.

They lined us up again. We waited for something to happen. I heard a loud thunderclap. Rain poured down from the sky. Well, I did want something to happen. The soldiers got out umbrellas. I thought they were going to hand them to us, but instead they would twirl the umbrellas in front us, taunting us that they were dry and we were naked and dripping wet. The rain quickly became ice droplets that pelted our skin.

We stayed outside in the drizzling rain for an hour or two and then two became four. My feet hurt from standing so long. I saw some women open their mouths for a drink. Soldiers walked up to them and hit their throats with their umbrellas. I automatically shut my mouth before they could get to me.

A group of soldiers walked by us. A soldier swaggered up to Emma and tickled her chin. She grimaced and he laughed and smacked her face. Anne glared at him. I tried to send her telepathic signals to stop or he'll see you.

She didn't get them.

The soldier noticed her hot glare. He walked to her and smacked her chest. She cried out and hit him back. He took a step back in shock. He yelled a few words that I couldn't understand and started beating her. He punched her face, stomach, and neck. She crumpled to a heap on the ground. I wanted to help her, but I couldn't do anything to save her. I was paralyzed with fear, astonishment, and horror. I stood still.

Emma stood still too. She looked ahead, biting her lip until tears came down her eyes. She squeezed her hands together. Mother couldn't stay still. She wanted to fight for her child like she had fought for Papa. She pulled the soldier off and held Anne in her arms.

Anne's face was bloody. Her eye swelled up and her nose bled profusely. The rain spread the blood all over her face. Her nose was crooked in an odd way. She groaned and moved her arms. She was still alive!

The soldier pulled Mother away. He dragged Anne towards his fellow soldiers. One handed him a hammer. This can't be happening. I need to stop this.

But I couldn't.

He took the hammer and raised it in the air. I screamed, "Anne, be strong. For Papa be strong! Be strong!"

She smiled weakly at me, "I'll see him soon."

It came down on her. The noise was indescribable. The soldier struck her five times. After each time, more of her brains flew out of her head. I vomited and fell to the ground. I felt Emma wrap her arms around me. I heard her crying in my ear. I heard Mother's painful wails.

My baby sister is dead.

I had promised to protect her. I didn't do anything. Anything! I remember first looking at her at the hospital. Mother had handed her to me and said, "Look, Jenna, you have a new baby sister. Say hi to Anne."

I remember her smile, that perfect, beautiful smile, and from that moment on I loved her. Papa had told me to not let anything happen to her, and I failed him. Why is this happening!?

I glared at the soldier who had taken her life. He sneered and dropped the hammer on the ground. He marched away with his pack of soldiers, leaving us with Anne's broken, dead body.

Chapter Four

We stood for another hour. They'd dragged Anne's body away. I'm glad they did. I couldn't bear to look at her any longer.

I remember teaching her how to braid her hair and how to write in cursive. Her penmanship was so nice. I remember when she had nightmares I would fix her a cup of warm milk and read her a story.

That was back in our old house. I miss that place. Our neighbors were nice and quiet. I remember each of us had a room to ourselves. My room was painted light blue, and my curtains were white and lacy. Grandma had helped me make them.

I felt tears stream down my face and wiped them. I looked at my hands. They were covered in my blood, sweat, and tears.

A soldier barked a few words at us. A man in a white coat walked to us. He held a green umbrella. He examined a few women, but when he got to me he gasped. He grabbed my hair and studied it. He grabbed my face and looked into my eyes. He was staring at them like they were completely foreign to him. He smiled and said, "Hello, my name Dr. Keptin. Are you Polish?"

He had a funny accent, and it was hard to understand him. I answered, "No I'm—"

He interrupted with a shout, "Well what are you girl?"

"Jewish. I'm a Jew!" I yelped.

He gasped again. He pulled my hair harder. He yelled for the blonde soldier to come over. They spoke for a while. A few more soldiers came to examine me. They pulled my hair harder, and yanked on my eyelids to make them open wider. It hurt so much that I let out a shriek. The blonde soldier glanced at me and yelled at the soldiers. They scattered away.

He walked back to Dr. Keptin. They talked even longer, glancing at me occasionally. The blonde soldier approached me. He was very tall and I had to look straight up at him. He bent down to my eye level. He touched my face gently and looked into my eyes. I could tell by the look on his face he was shocked to see the color. He touched my hair, running his hands through it. I studied his eyes. They made me feel so relaxed. I let myself smile. He scowled and backhanded me and I staggered backwards.

Keptin walked to me, "We are taking you to Dr. Vinkleman. He'll be very interested in you."

Two soldiers grabbed my shoulders and pulled me away. Emma gasped and Mother started bawling again. I looked at Emma. She gave me a small wave. I called, "Be strong and brave!"

She nodded and Mother crumpled on the ground again. I knew she didn't want to see another daughter die. A soldier kicked her and she fell to her side. I let out a shout. I twisted out of the soldiers' grip and ran to her. I felt them grab my hands again and pull me away.

The soldiers carried me to a building hidden by bushy evergreen trees. We walked inside the building and I immediately felt the warmth. It felt so incredible. It smelled very clean and it looked very clean.

One soldier called, "Dr. Vinkleman? We have a new patient for you!"

A door swung open, and a couple of nurses shuffled out. One nurse pushed a shriveled girl in a wheelchair. Her hair was brown and crinkly. Her hands had little specks of red on them and it looked like blood. What scared me the most was that she had no eyes, only empty sockets. I saw a girl identical to her come out in a wheelchair. She had the same brown, crinkly hair, and she didn't have eyes either. Another nurse followed behind carrying a jar in her hands. It contained two pairs of blue eyes. I felt faint. Eyes in jars? What's going on here?

I saw a man in a white coat come out of a room with blood stains all over his gloved hands, "Yes?"

Seeing the blood made me panic. I started to scream and kick. If this is where I'm going to die, I'm not going out without a fight! I am not going to be one of the eyeless girls! My blood will not be splattered all over his gloves!

The soldiers wrestled me to the ground. A nurse wheeled in a wheelchair for me. I kicked it away. I heard them chase after it, cursing at me. I didn't know I could kick that hard! I elbowed a soldier in the nose. He grabbed his nose in pain. I wrestled my arm from the other soldier and made a mad dash for the exit door. The door opened, and I ran straight into the blonde soldier. I tried to turn around, but he already had his arms around me.

He placed me in the wheelchair. I kicked and squirmed trying to escape. He stood in front of me. His blue eyes were so hypnotizing that I stopped struggling. He was so tall and had a stern, yet gentle look on his face.

The nurses quickly strapped me into the wheelchair. Dr. Vinkleman examined me. He wasn't as hypnotizing as the blonde guard. He was much older looking. He had grey hair and watery blue eyes. Wrinkles took over most of his face. He touched my hair and I glared at the blonde soldier. I hate it when people touch my hair now. He seemed to nod his head, as if he understood me.

Dr. Vinkleman flashed a flashlight into my eyes. I squinted and blinked a few times. He nodded his head, "No twin?"

The soldier spoke up, "We didn't find one with her."

He nodded, "Hm . . . Yes, I like this one. I'll take her."

I squirmed more in my chair. I thought if I just wriggle out of these binds I could escape faster than . . . wait then what? Where would I go if I could escape? How could I get away from these people? I felt incredibly powerless.

I turned my attention toward the blonde soldier. He had a small smile on his face and a big dimple on his right cheek. That made me smile, but I instantly flinched. Last time I smiled at him he slapped me. A nurse pulled a syringe out of her pocket, "This'll hurt . . . a lot, but at least you'll stop trying to escape."

I felt the panic rise up in me. He smiled a little more. Wow! He was really smiling at me. Was he smiling because of the look of fear I have on my face? The dimple grew bigger. I heard myself belt out a laugh.

She injected it into me and I blacked out.

Chapter Five

I woke up on a bed in a small room wearing a green hospital gown. I hugged my new clothes, happy that I finally had something to wear. I sat up quickly, instantly regretting it. I flopped back down on the bed. I still felt dizzy from the shot.

The last thing I remembered was the blonde soldier staring and smiling at me. I remember laughing really hard that he had a dimple. I don't know why that struck me as funny though.

I tried sitting up again. I sat up slowly and looked around the room. There was a bookshelf and a wardrobe to the left of the door. Only a clock adorned a wall. It was a very plain and simple room.

Back at our old house, we had family pictures all over the house. My favorite was our family portrait. I remember Mother buying us all new dresses. Mine was light green and fit me well. Anne's dress was bright red and Emma's was a deep blue. Mother wore a deep purple dress, and Papa got a new suit. I closed my eyes, trying to remember what it looked like. I remember Emma complaining she looked ugly and weird. I loved my smile in the picture. I looked so grown up for a 14 year old.

A nurse opened the door, interrupting my thoughts. She had blonde hair and wore a lot of makeup. She also smoked a cigarette. When she talked she blew smoke everywhere, "I'm . . . ooh . . . Nurse Agnes. Mmm I'll be . . . oh . . . giving mmmyou . . . ooh . . . yourmmm shots."

She pulled a small table inside. There were so many syringes on the table. I laughed nervously, "Do I get all of those?"

She wiped my arm with alcohol. She jabbed a needle in and I squealed. She yanked it out, "One down, nineteen to go!"

"Nineteen?" I squeaked.

After every shot, she blew smoke directly in my face. I coughed and hacked to clear my throat. I saw a clock hanging by my bed. It was 10:32 a.m. My stomach groaned. Nurse Agnes heard it, "Sounds . . . ooh . . . like you mmmvant something to eat. You . . . . ahh . . . hungry?"

I almost asked if she was kidding, but I bit my tongue. I just nodded my head. She chuckled, "Mmm a few more shots and . . . ah . . . I'll get you something tommm eat."

Four shots later, she left to get my meal. I lied down on my back. My arms were stinging. My eyes watered from all the smoke that was blown into my face and I kept coughing. I took a short nap. I woke a few minutes later scratching my arms. It felt like I had mosquito bites!

I heard a knock on the door. Nurse Agnes brought in a tray of food. She sat it down next to me on the bed. I couldn't believe what was in front of me. Mashed potatoes, a slice of bread, and water; it looked incredible. I wanted to cry. At home, I ate huge meals with my family. We had parties and feasted like kings. Now I'm excited over a sliver of bread and mashed potatoes. I ate the food slowly, relishing every bite.

Nurse Agnes spoke, "I know the food here isn't . . . ahh . . . great, but you . . . ooh . . . learn tommm get used to it."

I bet she gets even better meals than me. I wonder what Emma and Mother are eating, or if they are even being fed. Nurse Agnes made me stand by the bare wall so she could take a picture of me. I didn't smile. After the picture, she left me in the room by myself. I took a small nap, enjoying the feeling of food in my belly.

I woke up and checked the clock. 11:45 a.m. I looked at the door. I contemplated if she locked it. I tip-toed to the door and slowly turned the knob and it opened! I poked my head around the door. The hallway was empty. At the end of the hall was a door. Could it be the door out of here? I stepped out of my room. The floor in the hallway was like ice! I slowly crept down the hall, checking behind me every few steps to make sure no one was following—

"Hey there!"

I yelped and whipped around. A skinny boy with short, black hair and granny apple green eyes smiled at me. He wore a long, green gown identical to mine. He repeated, "Hey there!"

I looked around. No one was in the hall but us. He gave me a concerned look, "Do you not speak Dutch? Oh, are you Polish?"

I glanced at him and answered, "I can speak Dutch. I'm Jewish"

He laughed, "Ok, well you didn't answer me before!"

I groaned, "Fine. Hi."

He smiled, "Much better. So are you trying to sneak out of here or something?"

I asked hesitantly, "You don't work here do you?"

He laughed, "Nope! I'm a patient like you. My name is James, what's yours?"

"Jenna. I'm trying to get out of here," I said quickly. "So it was nice meeting you. Goodbye!"

I turned around. A boy with short, black hair and granny apple green eyes stood in front of me. I thought James was behind me! How'd he get in front of me so fast? I stumbled backwards into someone. I turned around, "Oh I'm sorry!"

James smiled back at me, "You're ok!"

I whipped back to the front. The boy in front of me laughed, "Ha-ha! You must be confused. My name is Jacob."

I turned back around. James smiled, "He's my brother. We're twins."

Chapter Six

"You're . . . twins?" I gasped. Jacob stood next to James. They were identical.

James nodded, "Yep. I'm a minute older."

Jacob protested, "No! Only 52 seconds!"

James rolled his eyes, "Anyway, where is your twin?"

"I don't have one," I answered.

James frowned, "You don't have a twin?"

I shook my head no. Jacob raised his eyebrows, "So you don't have a twin and you're Jewish?"

I nodded, "Is that a problem?"

Jacob shook his head, "No, it's just . . . you are—"

"Blonde," finished James. "And blue eyed."

I nodded, "I got it from my grandma. The rest of my family has black hair and green eyes."

"It is very rare for a Jewish girl to have blonde hair and blue eyes," commented Jacob. "No wonder Dr. Vinkleman is interested in you."

I remember the man with the bloody hands. I shuddered, "He's kinda scary looking."

James laughed, "Scary? The Doc? He's so nice! Every time I see him I get a piece of candy. He's always checking in on all the patients here."

"He had bloody hands! You should've seen him!" I protested. "He was doing surgery or something!"

Jacob gave me a puzzled look, "He doesn't do that stuff. He only checks up on us. Usually we get shots and they really hurt! Sometimes you get sick, but most recover. We don't have surgeries here."

I insisted, "There were these two girls and both didn't have their eyes! They were put in a jar! The girls had crinkly, brown hair. The eyes were blue."

James frowned, "Samantha and Alice have crinkly, brown hair and blue eyes. Do you know where they are, Jacob?"

Jacob shook his head, "No. Didn't they get really sick the other day?

Sam was throwing up blood and Alice was so hungry she started eating it. It was so nasty! I heard they were sending them to the camps since they couldn't use them anymore."

Use them for what? I felt a sharp pain in my arm, "Ouch!" I grabbed by right arm.

James looked at me in surprise, "Are you ok?"

I groaned, "I had 20 shots today."

Jacob laughed, "You're lucky you're new. I only had 35 today. James had 36. I guess they prefer the younger ones right, James?"

James glared at his brother, "Right. You get used to them after a while. The longer you're here the more they give you. That's probably the only downside of being here. You should get a cloth wrapped around that."

I led the boys back to my room. James searched my drawers for a cloth. He found a ribbon and wrapped it around my arm. Jacob explained, "Usually they give you a special wrap. Gauze, I think."

"Nurse Agnes was smoking too much to pay attention I guess," I said, rolling my eyes. "Although she did get me some food and it tasted so good!"

Jacob asked, "Do you still have any family?"

"Jacob!" scolded James. He looked apologetically at me. "I'm sorry if you lost someone. My idiot brother doesn't have manners. You don't have to answer that question."

I smiled, "It's fine. I have two sisters, my papa, Mother, and grandparents. My sister, Anne, and my papa were killed by the soldiers, and my grandma died last winter of pneumonia."

"I'm sorry for your losses," Jacob said sheepishly. "I didn't mean for my question to sound like that."

I smiled, "It's ok. How long have you been here?"

"A couple weeks," Jacob answered.

"It's nice having someone new here," James said with a smile.

"Are there not many kids here?" I asked. "Or are they all much younger than us?"

Jacob shook his head, "It's not that. Kids here just don't stick around for very long."

"And not all of them are very nice," James added. How long do they stay then? I wanted to ask that, but my stomach interrupted me with a loud growl. James chuckled, "Good thing it's lunch time. Do you want to join us?"

"Sure!" I replied. I followed them out of my room. For the first time, I'm making friends, and with boys at that! Maybe this hospital isn't that bad. I was practically starving to death when I got here. Perhaps the girls were part of my imagination, along with the blonde soldier smiling at me.

The hallway was really long. There were many rooms along the way. It reminded me of a hotel I stayed in with my family on a vacation. It was a big, fancy hotel. I was only 10, but I remember it was a lot of fun. However, there were many differences between the hotel and this hospital. The floors in this part of the hospital were covered in dirt and dust and yellow stains. Is that poop? There were little specks of red on a door. Is that blood?

James took my hand. When I looked at him, he had a grin on his face, which contrasted with my scared look, "I want you to meet some of our friends! They're really cool, trust me."

He led me into a room. Two boys sat on different beds. They were really skinny. They looked up at us in sync. James introduced them, "That is Kevin on the left and Devin on the right. Guys, this is Jenna and she's new here."

Kevin and Devin waved and said hello. Both boys had blonde hair. Kevin had brown eyes, but Devin had one brown and one blue.

I asked, "Devin, why is one of your eyes brown and the other blue?"

He shrugged his shoulders, "It just changed after I had an appointment with Dr. Vinkleman."

"What'd he do?" I asked.

"I don't really remember. I remember he gave me a shot. I woke up here. I noticed my eye color changed." He shrugged his shoulders. "Maybe they're changing colors. My allergies must be acting up though because they are so irritated!"

Kevin patted his shoulders, "You might be reacting to a shot. It'll be fine. They'll stop after a while."

I'm positive that the shot did it. Eyes don't naturally change colors and especially from a dark brown to a bright blue. A nurse walked in and smiled at us, "Children, you should go eat lunch. Devin, Dr. Vinkleman wants to see you again."

Devin followed the nurse out. Kevin walked with us to the cafeteria. I squeezed James's arm, "He wants to see him to check on his eyes. He changed his eye color! He's probably going to change his other one!"

He looked at me as if I had sprouted a second nose, "Jenna, Dr. Vinkleman doesn't do that. I don't know if *anyone* does that! Maybe Devin's eyes are hazel. Sometimes hazel eyes change colors."

"They brainwashed you. All of you!" I protested. I moved in front of him. "Don't you see what he's trying to do? He's trying to make perfect clones! He wants *everyone* to have blonde hair and blue eyes!"

"What did you say?" a timid voice asked.

I whipped around to see a little girl standing in front of me. She had beady, blue eyes and a little mouth. She wore a blue hospital gown that was two sizes too big for her. She had to have been six years old at least. What shocked me the most was that she had no hair on her head. I could tell that her hair was blonde because she had blonde eyelashes and eyebrows.

I tried to regain control in my voice, "I said that Dr. Vinkleman is experimenting on us. It's like he wants to make everyone look the same."

When she smiled, I noticed a few of her teeth were missing, "That's what I thought you said, and I think so too. He shaved my head for my blonde hair. It used to be as long and pretty as yours. I miss it." She rubbed her bald head. "I've seen some pretty strange things around here too."

I patted her shoulder, "I'm sorry about your hair. Do you really believe me about the doctor?"

She nodded, "Oh yes! In fact, I think they're trying to get my eyes next! I won't let them though! He can't have Annabelle back. Never!"

James stepped between us, "Go to lunch, Mallory. Scram!"

She shrieked and ran away. I glared at James, "Hey, she wasn't doing anything wrong."

He pulled me to the stairs, "Mallory is a crazy, little girl. Don't talk to her."

"But she believed me!" I protested.

Jacob mumbled, "Well she's crazy enough to."

I let that comment slide. I pulled my arm away from James, "When do I get to see the doctor?"

He answered, "Very soon. A nurse usually finds you when he wants to see you."

We walked into the cafeteria. James and Jacob helped me get food since my arms were still sore. They gave me a small turkey sandwich. There was barely any turkey in it, only cold bread. I never felt so happy to have food in my life. Even if it was just a meager sandwich!

We sat down together. I looked around the cafeteria and all I saw were extremely skinny kids. They were wolfing down their sandwiches, as if it were their last meal. For some it may be and they just don't know it.

Some of the kids were bald like Mallory. Others had different colored eyes like Devin. One girl had only one arm. Her gown covered her right stump. She held her sandwich in her left hand, chewing slowly and staring at her tray solemnly.

Two girls sat next to me. They were identical twins. They both had blonde buzz cuts and big blue eyes. Both were scary skinny. I'm sure they were my age too. Their names were Kristen and Kelly, and I forgot who was who.

One of them, I think she's Kelly, said, "Oh, your hair is so pretty!"

I smiled, "Thank you, Kelly."

Kelly smiled brightly. Whew! I got the correct name! Kristen sighed, "I remember when our hair was that long. I miss it so much."

Kelly explained, "We both got a bad case of lice. They shaved our heads, but it's growing back!"

Kristen crossed her arms and mumbled, "Barely."

Kelly asked, "Do you have a twin?"

I replied, "No. I had a younger sister named Anne, but she's dead. I have an older sister named Emma."

Kristen frowned, "Oh, I'm so sorry! We had two older sisters. Kaitlynn didn't make the ride here, and a soldier beat Kristina to death. She wouldn't get off the train. He kicked her head on the train tracks. It was the saddest day of my life"

I felt sick and not from the story. I felt woozy, and I wanted to lie down. It must be the shots. Oh, what did they inject me with?

I looked at James and Jacob. They ate their sandwiches normally. Is this common? Exchanging death stories? I said sympathetically, "Oh, I'm sorry for your losses!"

Kelly shrugged and looked down at her sandwich, "Yeah."

James smiled, "Hey, girls look at this!"

We turned to look at him. He had balanced his tray on his head. I glanced at Kristen and Kelly. They were cracking up with laughter. James looked right at me. I smiled and laughed. A goofy smile spread across his face and the tray tumbled off his head, which made us laugh harder. He smiled and looked down sheepishly.

Jacob applauded and we joined. Jacob took the tray from him and said, "Well done, brother, now step aside and let me show you how it is done!"

He set the tray on his head and let go. He smiled and winked at us and we clapped. He slowly stepped onto his chair. He lifted his hands up dramatically. Everyone in the cafeteria started laughing and clapping with us. He stepped down from the chair. James bowed to him and he bowed back.

"Shall I curtsey, your highness?" asked a small voice.

Jacob jumped and the tray clattered to the floor. I leaned over to see who was behind him. It was little Mallory. James glared at her, "Mallory, go somewhere else."

She frowned and stomped away. Kristen and Kelly gave her a look of disgust and so did Jacob. I asked, "Why do you guys hate her so much?"

James sat down and explained, "Well, she used to be a sweet, innocent girl. She also used to have an identical twin. Her name was Annabelle. Of all the kids here, Annabelle was Dr. Vinkleman's favorite. He always gave her candy, and she barely got any shots. No one really knew why she was so special to him and that drove Mallory crazy."

Kristen took over, "One day, Mallory was so upset because she had 23 shots in one day and she felt so sick. Meanwhile, Annabelle was happily babbling about her day. Mallory grabbed a syringe and stabbed Annabelle with it. I don't know what was in the syringe, but Annabelle died from it."

Kelly finished, "Dr. Vinkleman was so mad when he found Annabelle. He tried to save her, but he couldn't. Mallory became really crazy. They gave her special drugs so she wouldn't hurt anyone. She's psychotic! No one likes her because of what she did."

I asked, "Why is she still here?"

James said, "She's been here the longest; a whole year."

Kristen laughed, "Rumor was that Dr. Vinkleman wants to clone Mallory so he can have Annabelle back."

That explains why Mallory had shouted, "You can't have Annabelle!"

Kelly pushed her sister and said seriously, "Well they still need her for all the research!"

I frowned, "Research?"

Jacob replied excitedly, "Yeah, we're here so they can make new medicine. We're the guinea pigs! They use us to test new vaccines and medicines. Completely safe though. It's better than being out there in the concentration camps. At least we are helping others get better! It's definitely safer than being in those camps."

"Is it safe? What about Samantha and Alice? Didn't they get sick?" I asked.

"We get sick all the time, but I'd rather get the shivers and throw up occasionally then to be out there in the camps," Kelly shuddered. "I heard that they throw people who live more than two weeks into the gas chambers."

Kristen nodded, "I heard that they throw you in freezing water and see how long you last. I wouldn't last a minute; I can't swim!"

James said, "You'll like it here, Jenna, I promise. A few shots here and there, but you have us!"

Jacob added, "Yeah, we're not having eye surgery or anything like you said."

"Eye surgery?" asked Kristen and Kelly.

I shrank back into my seat. I felt really silly. Only crazy Mallory believes me, but I won't stop investigating this. I said, "I want to believe you guys, but you didn't see what I saw when I first got here."

James shook his head, "You were scared, malnourished, and probably a little crazy from being inside the train cars. I know I was. You probably imagined those girls."

"What girls?" Kristen asked.

I explained to her what I saw. Kristen gasped along with her sister. Jacob asked, "Have you girls seen Samantha and Alice?"

Kelly shook her head, "No. Weren't they going to send them to the camp after what happened? Seeing Alice eating Sam's vomit made me want to throw up. They're too sick to test on; they should go to the camp."

Everyone at the table turned silent. I poked my uneaten sandwich. Could I be right? Do I want to be right about this? I want to stay alive here. It was definitely better than being in the camp, besides the fact I don't know if Emma or Mother are alive. I wish I could see them again.

But is this safe? Alice and Samantha got extremely sick. All the other kids seem confident in the safety of the experiments being performed on them, or are they just terrified of the world out there and just want a meal and a safe place to stay?

Kristen finally spoke, "You know what? I haven't seen Jessica or her sister Jade in a few days either. In fact, a week ago their eyes looked different. Their eye color is gray, but it had changed to blue."

Everyone has a grim look on their face now. I felt bad, like I brought all this stress on them. I couldn't believe that they didn't even realize what was going on though.

"So what was the worst sickness you guys got from the tests?" I asked. I wanted to change the topic, but that's all I could think of.

Kristen smiled, "I remember I couldn't stop puking. I felt like my insides were getting cleaned out. I couldn't eat anything without it coming back up."

Kelly laughed, "Oh yeah? One time my face was totally white, and my teeth wouldn't stop chattering. I couldn't get out of bed. Do you remember that?"

Jacob said, "My worst was when I got 40 shots in a day. I started sweating and shaking. I felt my heart race and it wouldn't stop! Then, they gave me even more shots to make it stop!"

They continued to talk about their shots and symptoms. I was about to dig in to my microscopic sandwich when I felt a tap on my shoulder. I turned around. A nurse smiled down at me, "Hi, Jenna, Dr. Vinkleman is ready to see you."

My stomach protested, but I am anxious to meet him. Maybe I could find out more about his experiments. I followed the nurse downstairs.

James told me there are three floors to the building. The second and third housed the patients. I guess the first floor was mostly offices. His office is on the first floor, maybe along with surgery rooms?

She knocked on his door, "Dr. Vinkleman, Jenna is here to see you."

"Come in!" he called.

She opened the door and sent me inside the room. I saw the doctor sitting behind his desk. His office was really big. He had two chairs in front of his massive desk. Bookshelves and paintings were scattered around the room.

He was writing something. A death report? A failed experiment? He smiled and slipped the paper into his desk drawer. He gestured for me to sit down, so I did. He walked to a file cabinet and pulled out a file. He sat back down and put on his glasses. He glanced up at me, "So, Jenna, I see you are Jewish. That is a surprise to me."

"Why is that?" I asked.

"It is rare for a Jew to have blonde hair and blue eyes."

"Is that so?" I retorted. I wanted to stay cool, calm, and collected.

He stood up and walked to the chair next to me. He sat down, "Jenna, I want a closer look at your eyes. Lean towards me."

I leaned toward him. He touched my face and stared at my eyes. He felt my hair too, stroking it softly. He made a few notes in his notebook. He asked, "Do you have a twin that I don't know of?"

I answered, "No. Why am I here if I don't have one? Everyone else here has a twin."

He smiled, "Not everyone. You just got here you don't know everyone."

"But why am I here? Why are all of us here?" I asked.

He smiled again, "You are too valuable to be working out there. Everyone here has something special about them. All I am doing is using the healthiest children to test simple vaccines."

I asked, "Do you specialize in anything? Like surgery perhaps? Eye surgery?"

He stood up quickly, "I'm going to give you a couple of shots."

"I've already had 20 shots today!" I protested.

He walked to his desk and rummaged through his drawers. He muttered and slammed the drawers shut. He looked at me, "I'll be right back. Stay put."

He left the room. I waited a few seconds before I ran to his desk. I tugged on his drawers, but they were locked. I looked at his messy desk. I tried to read some of the documents, but they were in German. I wish I knew that language.

I walked to the cabinet where he got my file. I quickly thumbed through some of the files and I came across both Jacob's and James's file. I opened James's file first. He looked so sad in his picture. His face was scarred and his hair was messed up. He looked even skinnier then.

I tried to read the doctor's handwriting. It wasn't in German; it was Dutch. It's really sloppy and in cursive.

I put his down and opened Jacob's. He actually smiled in his picture. It really didn't look too bad. The handwriting in his was different. It's small, but very neat. I could easily read it. I skimmed through it. I saw something that made me drop the file. I almost screamed.

At the bottom of his file it said: *Take out eyes and replace with twin James's next week.* It had a date on the file, but I'm not sure what today's date is. I looked up at a calendar on the wall. The doctor put x's on the days that have past. Oh no! They plan on taking Jacob's eyes out tomorrow!

Chapter Seven

I heard Dr. Vinkleman's footsteps coming down the hall. I grabbed all the papers and shoved them back into the folder. I placed the folder back in the cabinet and ran to my seat. He walked in as soon as I sat down. He had three syringes in his hands. He instructed me to stand up, so I stood. He pulled my gown up, and automatically I flinched. It felt weird for a grown man to pull my clothes up.

He injected the needle into my lower back. It didn't hurt too badly, but it made my back numb. He injected the next one and it stung. I groaned and fell to my knees. I couldn't control myself. My legs felt funny. The last one came, but I couldn't feel it.

A nurse came and escorted me to my room. I felt woozy, and the room was spinning. I saw food on a tray by my bed, but I ignored it. I flopped on the bed and was out like a light.

I woke up feeling sore. I could barely feel my legs. I sat up stiffly and checked the clock. 7:30 a.m. I suddenly remembered the files I read yesterday. Jacob will lose his eyes today. I need to warn him and James. I struggled out of bed. My legs were stiff and rigid. What did that man give me?

I stood up and threw up all over my floor. My head exploded in pain. Whoa! I flopped into my mess. The smell reminded me of the train car when Anne threw up in my lap. I crawled to the door and pulled myself up using the door knob. I opened the door and stumbled out.

Where is their room? I kicked one foot in front of the other. Why can't I move my legs? My breath became panicky huffs. I felt my stomach lurch again, and I fell to the ground. I cried out in pain.

A nurse walked out of a room. She saw me crumpled on the ground. She ran to my aid and helped me back to my room. She practically carried me there. She asked, "What's wrong?"

"My . . . legs," I gasped. I couldn't move them anymore.

She helped me into bed, "Calm down. You're reacting to some of the shots they gave you."

My hands were shaking. I felt so sick. I wanted to vomit, but there was nothing left in my stomach. My chest throbbed as if my heart wanted to pop out, "H-help m-m-me!"

"Hm, a shot of—"

"No more shots!" I screamed. My arms began to shake uncontrollably. The nurse ran back out into the hall. I saw flashing colors. I was sweating and breathing hard. My head started spinning, or is that just me twisting my neck side to side?

She came back with Dr. Vinkleman. He checked my pulse and nodded. He looked at the nurse, "I want to see if she can survive this dose. She is very strong . . . and stubborn. If she doesn't make it . . . well she knew too much anyway."

She nodded, "Yes, Dr. Vinkleman."

He winked at me. I glared back at him. I wanted to say something, but my throat was on fire. I felt like if I spoke I'd spit flames. Maybe I could singe his eyebrows. The nurse strapped me to my bed.

"Strap them tight. Send Nurse Agnes up to feed her. She can't move from this spot. Understood?" commanded Dr. Vinkleman.

She nodded and left. He followed her out. I heard him say, "Send Jacob to my office. We need to begin the extraction."

I let out a moan. I struggled with the binds, but it was no use. I was stuck here, just like when Anne died. I had stood still, and now I can only lie still while Jacob loses his eyes. I suddenly felt drowsy. I felt like I had anvils strapped to my eyelids. I drifted to sleep.

I heard a knock at my door, "Jenna, it's Nurse Agnes. I brought you lunch."

She opened the door and shuffled inside. She wasn't smoking this time. She set a tray of food down. I was hungry, but I didn't want anything from her. I definitely didn't want to look at her. She worked for that evil doctor. She touched my head, "Are you awake? Are you ok? You're burning up! Maybe I should get the doctor."

My throat didn't hurt as much so I yelled, "No! No! No! I'm fine. Perfect!"

She took a step back in shock. She mumbled something I couldn't hear. I saw her head hover above mine, "Look, you need to eat. Open wide."

I opened my mouth and tasted cold pasta. I wanted to spit it out, but I chewed and swallowed. I cleared my throat, "I'm not hungry. Stop!"

Another fork full of food went into my mouth. She chuckled, "Nonsense. You need to eat to keep your strength up."

"Why should I? I don't do anything here. No one does. I'll just throw it back up anyways!"

She sighed, "Fine but you know you can't get up right? I'll be here until you finish this pasta."

I grumbled and ate another bite of pasta, "What did they give me?" She wouldn't answer me. Fine, I won't eat then. She tried to get me to open my mouth again, but she failed. I wouldn't open up my mouth. After a few more tries, she gave up and left the room.

I grunted trying to wriggle out of my bonds. My chest, wrists, waist, knees, and ankles were bound by leather straps. It was impossible to move. To make it worse, I had no feeling in my legs!

Suddenly, my stomach lurched and my lunch flew out. I stifled a cry. I licked a noodle from my cheek. I closed my eyes and tried to wake up from this terrible nightmare.

I woke up hours later. I heard a tap on the door. I twisted my head, "Come in!"

James walked into my room. I felt like someone kicked me in the stomach. I didn't want him to see me like this. He smiled at me, "Hello, Jenna." He saw my messy face and restraints. "Whoa, what'd you do?"

"James," I said weakly. My throat was so scratchy and dry. "Water."

He picked up a glass from the tray, "Here, drink it . . . are those noodles all over you?"

I gulped it readily. Suddenly, my throat closed up and I choked. James panicked and tried to lift me to pat my back, but he couldn't undo the restraints. I coughed harder until I felt my throat open. I sucked air in and began to breathe normally. I looked at him and said, "Ok. I'm ok now."

His eyes were still wide with fear. He asked, "What did you do? I've never seen anyone in the restraints on the bed."

"James, I need to tell you something," I said slowly. I didn't want to get excited and throw up again. "I was in Dr. Vinkleman's office. He left the room, and I went to his cabinet full of files. I found yours and Jacob's."

"Jenna, you can't do that," he said in a stern whisper. He paced the room and glared at me. "Why would you do that? Dr. Vinkleman is a good man and I don't know why you—"

"I read Jacob's file," I interrupted. "I saw something in it, something awful."

James stopped. He looked at me. He had a hint of fear on his face,

"What?"

"It said they were taking his eyes out today and then replacing them with your eyes next week."

James stepped back. He had a shocked look on his face. He said grimly, "Are . . . are you sure? Don't lie to me."

"I'm not lying I swear."

He held his head in his hands. I saw tears water up in his eyes. He murmured, "It all makes sense now. You were right. I should've listened."

I felt a tear go down my cheek, "Where is he, James?"

James looked into my eyes. He said solemnly, "A nurse took him to Dr. Vinkleman. I wondered why she took him because I always go in the morning and he goes in the afternoon on certain days."

I struggled with the binds, "We need to stop them! We can make it if we hurry!"

He pulled on the leather straps. He yanked the one restraining my upper body free. I flexed my hands and pulled on the other straps. Finally, I was free. He helped me up. I still felt weak, and I couldn't move my legs very fast. I wiped my face with the sleeve of my gown and told him, "I can't move very fast."

He wrapped his arm around me, "I've got you. Let's go save my brother."

We stumbled down the hall to the staircase. Well, he dragged me down the hall to the staircase. My legs couldn't keep up with the rest of me. I looked at James. He had a determined look on his face. He glanced at me, "I'm sorry, Jenna, I should've trusted you."

"I wouldn't have trusted me either," I replied with a smile. "We can make it and Jacob will be fine."

He nodded but I could still see the fear and doubt in his eyes. We made it to the first floor. I had an abrupt thought that if the nurses see us, we would be drugged so much we wouldn't wake up until Hanukah.

James pulled me behind a cart of syringes. He looked at me and said in a low voice, "Dr. Vinkleman's office is two doors down."

We made our way to his door. As James grabbed the door knob, the door suddenly flung open. Nurse Agnes was startled by us. She opened her mouth to scream, but James quickly pushed her into the office. I shut the door behind us. He shoved her into a chair. She began to wail, but he clamped his hand over her mouth. He looked at me and commanded, "Find Jacob's file!"

I stumbled to the cabinet. I leaned on it and searched for the file. I called, "It's . . . it's not here!"

He growled at Nurse Agnes, "Where is my brother?"

"I . . . I don't know!" she stammered.

He leaned closer to her, "You know. What is the doctor doing to him? Tell me!"

She squeaked, "Eye surgery. He's taking his eyes out to test them. He'll take yours next. He wants to put them back into your brother's eye sockets to test his new theory."

"What new theory?" I asked.

She looked at me curiously, "How'd you get out of your restraints?"

James hit the desk, making Nurse Agnes whip her head back to face him. He commanded, "Answer her question."

She took a few deep breaths then said, "Ok, I'll tell you. Dr. Vinkleman has been experimenting on kids, mainly twins. He wants to create the perfect race for Hitler, but so far his attempts have failed. Most children don't make it through the surgeries, but that doesn't stop him. He examines the eyes to see what makes them blue. He adds chemicals to the eyes to change their color. We give the kids drugs to put them to sleep so they won't remember what happened. He also tests vaccines and medicines for the government. He tests polio vaccines on kids and that's why you can't feel your legs, Jenna. You're lucky though; some kids get a really strong virus and a bad vaccine. I heard they didn't give you much of the virus to begin with. You'll just be a little sick and numb in the legs for a while."

I would hate to lose my legs. Would they be amputated? I could barely feel them, but it was better than not being able to feel them at all.

James asked, "Can we save Jacob?"

She shook her head, "He's already in surgery and he won't be coming back. If he makes it, they'll keep him in a special room until your surgery."

James threw his hands in the air. He started pacing, "But I'll notice my brother missing. What will they tell me?"

She said softly, "They will say that they don't need him here anymore. They're done researching on him and they sent him to the camp to work."

James nodded, "Like Samantha and Alice right?

Nurse Agnes started to cry, "Not exactly. They have never sent anyone back to the camp. They strip their flesh away to collect their skeletons for a collection. I only tell kids that so they don't know that their siblings are now part of a gruesome collection. Samantha and Alice . . . unfortunately are now."

He stopped pacing. He gazed at Nurse Agnes. He whispered, "Really?"

She nodded, "Yes. I'm sorry."

He plopped to the ground. He buried his face into his hands and sobbed. I sat down next to him to comfort him. I hugged him, "I'm so

37

sorry, James."

He muffled, "No, Jenna, I'm sorry. I should've listened to you. If I had, I would still have my brother."

"Don't talk like that. Maybe he'll make it, and he'll come right back to you," I said reassuringly. I looked at Nurse Agnes. "Do they survive the surgery?"

She shook her head, choking on her tears, "No. There is a slim chance of survival."

Chapter Eight

Nurse Agnes escorted us back to our rooms. She gave me a new blanket to sleep on and a clean gown. I lied down on the bed. Papa was dead. Anne was dead. Jacob was probably dead. Mother and Emma are fighting for their lives in the camp, and who knows if they're dead. James will have his eyes taken out next week, meaning he may die too. How long do I have? I've never thought about how I'm going to die, but getting my eyes yanked out by a sadistic doctor is not the way I had imagined I would go.

James walked into my room. He had a file in his hands. He looked at me with a grim expression and said, "I need to show you something. I stole your file from the cabinet in his office and don't worry the nurse didn't see me."

I patted the spot next to me. He sat next to me and handed me the file. I saw my picture. I looked so sick. The gash on my forehead was oozing pus. I touched my forehead. I never knew it was that bad. It was now a long scab. I opened the file. I didn't have much since I've only been here for two days.

I squinted at the handwriting. It's in German. I passed it back to James, "I don't know German. Can you read it to me?"

He began, "Well basically it says you were malnourished when you got here and most of us were. Overall, you are very healthy. It has a record of all the shots they gave you. The first twenty you got were little viruses. It says you didn't have much reaction. Oh, here are the last three: one of them is a polio vaccine, the other is the polio virus, and the last one is morphine. That's a sleeping drug I suppose."

"Ok," I said, rubbing my legs. They wouldn't stop throbbing. I guess it's better to feel pain in them than to not feel them at all.

He pointed at a sentence at the bottom of the page, "This says, *shave head for hair samples. Consider eye surgery or eye drops.* It doesn't have a date when to do it though."

I felt my mouth drop. This can't be happening. I touched my hair. Why do so many people want it? I blinked out a tear. Why do so many people want my eyes? What is so special about them? Why am I so special to them?

I felt his gentle hand on my back. I hugged him and cried into his shoulder, soaking his hospital gown. He patted my shoulder, "I'm sorry, Jenna."

I lifted my head up to look at him, "Don't be, you're going through worse things. We don't know how Jacob is doing, or what will happen to you when they take you."

He looked into my eyes, "I want to live. Jenna, we need to get out of here. We need to escape."

The thought of it made me laugh, a boy and girl escaping from an experimental hospital in a concentration camp. It was impossible! James took it seriously though, "Why are you laughing? Do you want to lose your hair and eyes?"

"No I don't!" I snapped. "It's just the thought of escaping from a place like this and then trying to get out of a concentration camp just sounds impossible."

"I know," he said. "I think I have a plan. I could carry you—"

I laughed, "You can't carry me all across Europe. Who knows how long it's going to be until I can feel my legs? Maybe never!"

"Don't say that! Sometimes when I get shots, I get sick for weeks. Once I couldn't even get out of bed. One day Dr. Vinkleman came in and said I didn't have much longer to live. Jacob never left my side and helped me through it. We both helped each other through our sicknesses. I'll help you through this, Jenna. When you feel better, we can get out of here."

"What if as soon as I'm healthy, they inject something else in me? Or what if you get sick?" I asked.

"Lately the stuff they've been giving me hasn't made me too sick. One shot gave me a bad stomach bug, but I recovered pretty quickly," he said. "Jacob had it worse. They had given him eye drops before. It made his eyes water for days. I guess they were attempting to change his eye color. It didn't work obviously. Anyway, can you move your feet at all?"

I tried to wiggle my toes. The big toe moved slightly. The rest were still stiff. I said, "It'll be a while."

"That's ok. It will give me more time to think about how to escape," he smiled. "You're probably one of the toughest girls here. The toughest girl I've ever met. You can survive this."

I smiled and hugged him. Nurse Agnes walked into the room. I shoved the file under my blanket. She didn't seem to notice. She paid more attention to the boy sitting on my bed with me. She cleared her throat,

"James, go to your room. A nurse is waiting with your shots."

He nodded and left. Nurse Agnes sat next to me, right on the file. It made a crackling noise. She pulled it out of the blankets and glared at me. I looked down at my feet. She sighed and pulled a cigarette out from her pocket. She lit it and stuck it in her mouth. She opened the file up, "Look . . . I know that youmm . . . probably want to leave this place, but . . . ooh . . . believe me you don't even knowmm what it's like living out there in the . . . ooh . . . camp. You'remmm lucky to be . . . hahm . . . here."

I snapped, "Lucky to be tested on? I will get my hair hacked off! My eyes will be removed! You think that's lucky?"

She glared at me, "Luckier than . . . ooh . . . the little Gypsy girls withmm no clothes on . . . ahh . . . standing outside by the crematories."

That shut me up, but not for long, "Why do you care? I mean, most of the nurses are nice, but all they want is our body parts! All they want to do is their job, but they aren't doing it right because no one is getting better here!"

She sighed and took the cigarette out of her mouth, "Let me tell you my story. I used to be a nurse at a hospital in Amsterdam called First United Hospital. I liked my job a lot. One day, they fired me because I gave a Jew treatment for a burn. I didn't even know she was Jewish. All I knew was that she needed my help. That's why I was there, to help people. After that, I lost my house because I couldn't make payments. My husband had already left me months ago, and my son joined the Nazi Party. He was so upset with me for helping that Jewish girl; he wouldn't let me stay with him. I took the job here. I got a little house here, I'm well fed, and I thought I would be helping children. However, I'm actually just making them worse."

She sniffled, wiping her nose. I felt bad for her so I patted her on the shoulder, "I'm sorry. You're the only nurse here who has actually listened to me and helped me a little. I would really like to be able to trust you."

She smiled, "Thanks! It feels nice to be trusted by someone."

I asked, "So were you always a smoker too?"

She laughed, "Oh, no. I just started this when I moved here. All the stress really builds up on a person. I heard smoking helps relieve stress. So far it's working pretty well."

I nodded, "So why did you come in here?"

She nodded, "I'm supposed to record how much movement you can make. Can you stand?"

I stood slowly, but lost my balance and fell back onto the bed. My legs felt like they were asleep. I stomped to wake them up, but my knees wouldn't bend. I felt like kicking in frustration, but all I could do was slightly twitch my right leg. She inhaled the smoke and wrote something down. I asked, "So how'd I do?"

She glanced at me and laughed, "Horrible. Mmmmhoney, it's gonna be . . . ahh miracle if you can stand in a week!"

A week? I hope James won't get too upset, but something else also worried me. "Nurse Agnes, it says on the file they're going to shave my head."

She nodded, "Yes they do that to the blonde ones . . . ooohhh . . . and a common case of lice."

I fiddled with my hands, "Oh, well, I don't want them to take it off."

She laughed, "So you think they'll listen to you and not do it? Ha-ha! Mmmmhoney you might as well kiss your hair goodbye because they will cut it. They don't take your thoughts into consideration."

I sniffled. That's what I'm worried about. She noticed my reaction and asked, "Why are you so worried about it? Most girls actually don't mind it after a while. We don't have showers for the kids here. Your hair will just get nastier. You might as well shave it off!"

"Yes but . . . my hair helps me remember my Papa," I whispered. "He loved my hair and eyes. He always told me that my eyes were bluer than the sky and deeper than the ocean."

She mumbled, "My father never told me stuff like that, but . . . ooohhh . . . I understand. However . . . ooohhh . . . I don't think the doctors will. All they care about is their research, and they'll rip and cut anything off you if it helps their research."

I shook my head, "I don't want my hair removed. Who does it anyway?"

She sighed, "Mmmwell, we nurses do it. I haven't yet."

I said, "Promise you won't take mine."

She stood up and said, "I promise."

I gave her a look. She gave me one back, "Hey I said I promised! I, Agnes Felicity Holmwell, promise to not ever cut your hair off."

I smiled and nodded, "Thank you, Nurse Agnes."

I woke up in the middle of the night. My whole body ached, and my sheets were soaked with what I hoped was sweat. I sat up slowly. There was a foul odor in the air. It came from my sheets. I groaned. I can't believe I wet the bed.

I wanted to get out of bed, but my legs restrained me from doing that. I cried out for help, but no one came. I sat in my own urine. It reminded me of being on the train car when I had soaked my gown. I let the tears spill down my cheeks.

I have a week. That's if my body can fix itself fast enough; that will be a miracle. It's a miracle I'm still alive. I wish I wasn't. I wiped my eyes. I can't believe I'm wishing I was dead.

I needed to get out of this bed. The stench made me feel nauseated. I lifted each of my legs and placed them on the ground. They still felt numb. I leaned forward and fell to my knees. I rolled over to my back. The smell wasn't so overwhelming anymore.

I stared up at the ceiling. Cracks ran all over it. Inside the cracks, I could see green mold. Ugh! I wonder what gets the kids sick here, the viruses or the mold.

James thinks we can escape. I don't believe that, especially with my bad legs. I can barely get out of bed! He has so much faith in me though. He thinks I'm so tough and strong when really I'm terrified and weak! All of this thinking exhausted my brain enough for sleep to take over.

I felt the daylight shine on my eyes. I cracked one open. I'm still on the floor. I heard a loud rapping on the door, "Jenna?"

Oh thank goodness it's James. I rolled over to look at the door, "Yes, James?"

He cracked the door open, but he didn't stick his head in, "Hey, I'm not used to going into a girl's room all the time. Uh . . . are you decent?"

I blushed. He was sweet. I looked down at my stained gown I really didn't want him to see me. I said, "I'm kinda messy right now. Do we get new gowns?"

He replied, "There should be some in your wardrobe."

The wardrobe is next to the door. It looked so far away. I used my arms to pull myself toward it. I felt so weak and dizzy. I'm so hungry. I let out a pitiful groan. James heard it, "You ok in there? Do you need my help?"

I answered weakly, "Yes."

He slowly opened the door. He looked at my bed with a hint of disgust. I saw him take a deep breath and instantly regretting it. His nose crinkled up, and he pinched his nose. He looked down at me sprawled out on the floor. I felt so weak and helpless as he carried me to my bed and placed me on the drier side.

He opened the wardrobe door and pulled out another gown. He tossed it to me, "I'll be outside, tell me when you're done. I'll take you to breakfast."

I took off my wet gown. I stared at my gaunt stomach. My ribs poked out like daggers. My stomach felt like it was nothing but a small hole. I remember the days I would stand in front of the mirror, wishing I was as skinny as Emma. Now I'm skinnier than her.

I changed gowns. I felt so much better. I ran my hands through my hair. It was really greasy and dirty. Oh, what I would give for a shower.

I called James back. He came in and helped me stand. I felt wobbly. I flopped back onto the bed, sighed and tried again and again. This is impossible. It feels like I will never be able to walk again.

I looked at James. He read the frustration in my eyes. He pulled me up and held me steady. He looked at me hard in the eyes, "You can do this. Just stand for five seconds."

1 . . . 2 . . . 3. I wobbled and fell into him. He pushed me back firmly. I waved my hands out to balance. 1 . . . 2 . . . back onto the bed. I shouted in frustration, "Just let me go! I want to stay here."

He laughed, "You kidding me? You need to eat. You need the energy to heal."

"Heal? Nurse Agnes said it will be a miracle if I get the feeling back in a week! I don't think I ever will. I might as well rot here in my room. Miracles don't happen."

"Don't say that! You will heal, you will walk, and you won't die! Now get up!" he commanded. He yanked me to my feet. I wobbled but stood firm. 1-2-3. My arms flapped wildly. He caught me and chuckled. "You looked like you were about to fly."

I'd like to fly as far from here as possible. I started to cry. I've cried so much these past few days I'm sure I could fill a bucket with my tears. James sighed and hugged me. He whispered, "What would Anne say to you right now? Give up? Or try harder? What would your Papa want?"

"H-he'd w-w-want me to b-be strong," I sniffled. "And b-b-brave."

"Then be strong and be brave," he said firmly. I let his words fill me up. I felt stronger and not as weak. I felt not just brave, but courageous. The feeling traveled through my legs. I felt myself soar higher. I stood up straight. James smiled and slowly let go of me. "One"

The feeling wavered. I felt weak; I wanted to fall back. I want to die. Why won't he leave me here? Why does he care?

"Two."

I can't believe I've stood by myself this long. Maybe I am a fighter. I'll do this. I'll do it for my family. For Papa and for Anne!

"Three."

My knees buckled. I fought back. I want to eat. I want to escape. I want to live. I want this for my family.

"Four . . . Five," I fell forward into his arms. He caught me, and I met his eyes. They were smiling with joy. He said. "Miracles clearly can happen."

Chapter Nine

James carried me down the hall. He told me how proud he was of my accomplishment today. He says he'll work with me every day to get my legs working. I felt so excited. I'm a fighter. I can survive; I will survive through this. I'll be better in no time, and then James and I will escape.

He stopped by Devin and Kevin's room and called out, "Hey guys you in?"

Kevin opened the door. Something about him looked different. His arms looked bigger, like he had lifted weights. He looked healthier too. He tilted his head and smiled, "James, why are you carrying Jenna?"

James put me down. I explained, "My legs aren't working well. They gave me a polio vaccine to test. So far, I'm actually doing pretty well. I stood for five seconds today!"

Kevin smiled wider, "That's great! Usually the virus that they give you is strong, and it infects you. My older brother, Levin, was given the virus, but the vaccine didn't work. As a result, he got polio."

I frowned, "Oh I'm sorry. Did he get better?"

Kevin shook his head, "He died."

I felt a hard lump form in my throat. My heart sank to my stomach and burned. James peered over Kevin's shoulder, "Where's Devin?"

Kevin sighed, "He's been going to Dr. Vinkleman a lot lately and so have I. We haven't received many shots. I've had about five so far this week, and Devin only had three. Dr. Vinkleman even prepared a feast for us to eat yesterday. He won't let us eat the cafeteria food. He's also made us exercise. It's like he's preparing us for some big test!"

I sucked in a sharp breath and glanced at James. He didn't return my look. What could that doctor be doing to them? What is he preparing them for?

I stared at Kevin's eyes. They used to be a dark brown. Now they were a bright blue. He kept blinking and rubbing his eyes as if they itched inside his eye sockets. I asked, "Aren't your eyes brown?"

He nodded, "They changed yesterday. A few hours after my appointment with Dr. Vinkleman, they started to itch. I checked in the mirror and saw that they were blue. So are Devin's eyes, it's weird."

"You don't remember how they changed?" James asked.

Kevin shrugged his shoulders. It was the shot. The shot made him forget everything Dr. Vinkleman did just like Nurse Agnes had said. I wonder if it was morphine like mine.

A nurse interrupted us, "Kevin, Dr. Vinkleman wants to see you."

He nodded and looked back at us, "Bye, Jenna! Bye, James! Say where's Jacob? He's always with you, James."

"Not sure, well we're going to the cafeteria. See you later, Kevin. Tell Devin I said hi!" James said quickly. He swiftly picked me up and carried me to the cafeteria.

As soon as we were out of earshot I asked, "You ok?"

James had a small tear forming in his right eye, "Yes, I'm fine."

I paused for a moment. Jacob was always at James's side. It must be hard on him not having him there. James shook his head, "I just can't be myself without him. I feel like I'm missing something, like I'm walking around with only one sock or shoe. I'm half a person without Jacob."

I asked, "What do you think he is preparing him for? Maybe it's eye surgery."

"Well since we are just learning about all this stuff, who knows all the operations Dr. Vinkleman has done," he said. "He changed Kevin's eye color. He took out Jacob's, Samantha's, and Alice's eyes. He shaved Mallory's head. He injects vaccines and viruses into kids."

I nodded. Who knows what this man is capable of? How sick and twisted he can be? We arrived in the cafeteria. He set me down at one of the tables, "I'll get your breakfast."

I smiled and said thanks. I looked around the cafeteria. The same crowd shuffled around on the tiled floor. Their skinny legs looked like they could snap at any moment. Being bigger was an honor here. The more meat on your bones the higher respect you get.

Kelly sat next to me. Her eyes wouldn't stop twitching back and forth. Her eyes were as big as pie pans. She wouldn't stop looking at the entrance to the cafeteria. I asked, "Is something wrong? Where's Kristen?"

She flinched when I spoke. She whispered, "Jenna, you're right. There's something weird going on here. Dr. Vinkleman personally came to our room and took her. He's never done that before, at least not to me or my sister. I-I heard him saying that she will do a new test for him and a few other kids here. He said that she and the other kids were very special for this test."

I held her hand to calm her down, "Do you know what test it is?"

She looked into my eyes. Her blue eyes danced across my face. They watered and a tear flowed down. She whimpered, "I don't know, but I'm so scared and worried."

She squeezed my hands and buried her head into my shoulder. She sobbed quietly. James sat down next to me. He mouthed, "Is she ok?"

I shook my head. I pushed her head up as gently as I could and tried to smile, "Maybe James and I could find out something. Would you like that?"

She ignored my question, "Do you think that they sent her to the camps? That they have done testing on her like with Sam and Alice? What will happen to me? I've never been without her! She's my twin; my other half!"

I heard James cough. I turned around to see him. He is trying to hide the expression on his face. He figured out what was going on. I looked back at Kelly. Tears were streaming harder down her face. I smiled, wiping them away, "Look, I'll try to find some things out, but do you really want to know?"

She gasped, "I want to know what they've done to her!"

I nodded, "Ok. I'll go with James after breakfast. Maybe we could ask the nurses or something."

She laughed, "Since when are you friends with the nurses? All of them are so mean to me."

We ate in silence. I wanted to talk to James to figure out what had happened to Kristen, but not in front of Kelly. I'm afraid if she found out what we were up to, she'd try to escape with us. Hopefully, Kristen will come back and all will be normal. Well, as normal as things can be here.

After breakfast, James carried me to his room. Kelly wanted to come with us. Fortunately, a nurse came to give her shots. I don't think I could fill Kelly in on everything I've learned here so far, and I don't think she'd quite understand it.

James set me on the bed. I noticed an empty bed on the other side of the room. The sheets were taken off and the pillow was missing. It was an empty cot, Jacob's bed. James began to pace, "Ok so Dr. Vinkleman took Kristen today?"

I nodded, "And a few other kids."

"What could he be planning?"

"She said that it was a new test that he wanted to try on her and the other kids. He said that they are very special for this kind of test. What could that mean?"

"I don't know. Do you think he might have written it in her file?"

"Should we go look?"

"We could try."

Nurse Agnes walked into the room. She said, "Now what are you two conspiring about now? Oh, never mind! I learned more news about Jacob."

"Did he make it?" James asked eagerly.

She shook her head, "No. I'm sorry, James."

He nodded and looked down for a minute. We stayed silent to honor Jacob. I broke the silence and asked, "Do you know why Dr. Vinkleman took Kristen and a few other kids today?"

She thought for a minute, "Kristen . . . who is her twin?"

I answered, "Kelly. They're both."

Nurse Agnes turned pale, "Oh no. I heard he wasn't going to do that one."

James asked, "What?"

Nurse Agnes turned away, "Did you know that there is a pool here? They put one in a couple of weeks ago. There was some talk about filling it up and . . . and running a few tests."

"What kind of tests?" James asked nervously.

"Tests to tell how long a human can last in freezing water. Since it is freezing outside, they thought about filling it up with water and seeing how long Jews could last in the bitter, cold water. They put the idea aside for a while, but now they brought it back up," she explained. "The Nazi Party decided to fund us for it. The pool is filled up now. I don't know why they picked those particular kids though. God bless their souls."

I gasped. James looked at me, "What is it?"

"I know why," I squeaked. My head is spinning again. I felt myself fall down. James ran to my side. Nurse Agnes hovered over me. My eyes felt heavy. I want to sleep so badly, but I have to tell them. I opened my mouth, but it suddenly felt dry. Curse these drugs. I whispered, "Kristen - can't - swim."

Chapter Ten

I felt someone gently nudge me. I woke up. I looked around. I was back in my room, but not in the hospital room. My *old* room! I sat up quickly. I saw my white lacy curtains and the comforting blue color of my walls. I wiggled my toes. My toes! I can feel my legs! Oh, what a relief this was just a nightmare!

I heard a familiar laugh. Anne ran into my room and playfully slapped my shoulder, "Come get me, Sleepy Head!"

She always called me that when I slept in for a long time. I jumped out of bed and chased her down the hall. My legs moved quickly trying to catch her. I never felt so happy to be chasing Anne. I chased her into the kitchen. I saw Mother making muffins. She smiled at me, "Morning, Sunshine."

I stopped in my tracks. She glanced at me curiously. I embraced her, "Morning, Mommy!"

She laughed, "Mommy? When was the last time you called me that? Are you alright, Jenna?" She felt my forehead. "You don't feel too warm."

I danced around, "I've never been better!"

Emma bumped into my flailing arms, "Watch it!"

I turned around. She was wearing a loose, flowery dress. She looked so beautiful, "Oh, Emma, you look lovely!"

She raised her eyebrows, "Uh . . . ok? You never say that."

I hugged her, "I wish I had said it more. Emma, you're beautiful, and I love you."

Anne came back, "Hey what's going on?"

I looked at Anne. She had a confused look on her face, but she still smiled. She smiled through everything. I walked to her and took her hand, "I love you, Anne. I want you to know that. I loved you ever since I first saw you."

She smiled wider and laughed, "Did you have a bad dream or something?"

I laughed along with her, "Oh, you'd never believe it."

I heard several loud knocks. I looked at the door. Could it be Papa coming back from work? Anne skipped over to answer it. As soon as she touched the knob, the door burst open. It smashed her underneath. Soldiers filed into the room. Mother shrieked and grabbed Emma and me. It's happening again!

A soldier grabbed my arms. I screamed and pushed him away, but he wouldn't let me go. I kicked and scratched him. He looked into my eyes. It was the blonde soldier. His eyes pierced into mine making me scream louder. He dragged me aside to watch the other soldier beat Emma and Mother. The blonde soldier kept whispering into my ear, "Jenna . . . Jenna . . . Jenna . . . Jenna."

"Jenna? Wake up, Jenna," James whispered.

I sat up quickly, knocking heads with him. He groaned and fell to the ground. I looked at him, "Oh, James, I'm sorry!"

He rubbed his head, "No, it's fine. Ow! You've got a hard head!"

I rubbed my head, "Sorry. Did I fall asleep?"

He nodded, "Right after you told us that Kristen can't swim, you passed out. I carried you to your room. Nurse Agnes brought you lunch in case you woke up. Dr. Vinkleman had come in to check on you too. He didn't inject you with anything. I had spied on him the whole time. He had only checked your pulse."

It was only a dream. I tried to wiggle my toes. The big toe shifted slightly and the rest twitched. No more chasing Anne or hugging Mother. No more admiring Emma or waiting for Papa to come home. All of that is now a faint memory; a memory that will only be real in my dreams.

James handed me a tray, "This is dinner; it's fish. I snuck you another piece too. You need to eat as much as you can to regain your strength. You're lunch is still here too and it's a sandwich."

I smiled, "Thanks for everything. I've never had someone take care of me the way you have."

"You are welcome. I can't think of anyone else I'd like to escape with," He blushed and looked down at his clasped hands. "Well you know . . . from here because it is awful, not like .. . well .. . uh you enjoy that fish ok? I'll leave you to rest."

He awkwardly walked away, almost bumping into the door frame. I couldn't help but chuckle. He was very sweet and cute. It's amazing I've found a crush in a horrible place like this. I couldn't even fall in love at my old home!

I slowly ate the fish. It wasn't too bad. It was just a little cold. I ate the sandwich too. My stomach sighed in pleasure. I finally felt full. I sipped my water. I hope it doesn't come back up.

I rested in bed for a bit. I wish I had a book to read or something to do to pass the time. I wonder what James is doing? I wish I could walk to his room to hang out with him. I wiggled my toes again. There was actually more movement.

I sat up. Maybe I could surprise him! I tried to move my legs so that they would dangle over the bed. They did it! I slowly shifted my weight onto my feet. My knees wobbled, but held strong.

It's time to take the first step. I lifted my knee, instantly regretting it. I lost balance and crashed to the ground. I stiffly got back up. Perhaps I should just shuffle my feet to his room. I barely bent my knees and shuffled my feet out the door. So far so good. I went down the hall. I remembered the way to his room so I shuffled down the hall, keeping my arms out for balance. This wasn't so bad. I got closer to Kevin and Devin's room. Maybe I'll come in and show them I can walk . . . sort of.

Suddenly, a loud wail pierced my ears. Was it a crazy kid? I panicked. What if the crazy kid was in the hallway? I knocked on the door, "Hey, boys, it's Jenna! Can I come in?"

The shrieking wail cracked and reduced to a moan. It came from their door. I heard loud steps come to the door. I shuffled back, almost tripping over my feet. The door cracked open. Kevin's head appeared. His eyes were wide and bloodshot. He was panting and crying.

I shuffled forward slowly, "Kevin? Are you ok? Is Devin there too?"

He clenched his fist, his eyes widened and his breaths came out in hard gasps. Kevin moaned in pain, and Devin's head popped up next to his head. Devin's face was red, and he wouldn't stop grunting and crying. Their faces were so close together.

Devin tried to say something, "Mjemmma! Je . . . jennn . . . oh!"

Kevin shouted, "We . . . we're . . . Sia . . . gah!"

Their faces disappeared. I opened the door wider, "Guys, are you al . ." My voice trailed off.

What I saw made me cry, scream, and vomit all at the same time. Kevin and Devin were joined together. Devin had his left arm and Kevin had his right arm. They shared the same torso. Bloodstains patched the gown that they shared. They looked inhuman. Their necks were crooked, and their heads wouldn't stop bumping together. They are Siamese Twins.

Kevin reached out for me. I stumbled back. They struggled to get closer to me. They couldn't work together very well. I screamed and scooted backwards. My screams combined with their moans attracted the nurses' attention.

"What's going on? Ahh!" shouted a nurse. She half carried half dragged me away from them.

The boys reached out for me, "No! Jee . . . Jeeennna!"

"No! Wait!" I yelped. They just wanted me to talk to them. I reacted poorly. "Wait! I'm sorry, Kevin and Devin! I'm sorry! Please stop I just want to talk to them!"

"Stop protesting!" demanded the nurse. Two nurses pushed the combined boys back inside the room. She dragged me to my room and set me back on my bed. "Stay in bed!"

I automatically sat up, "No! I want to talk to them. They're lonely and scared! Did you not see them?"

She snapped, "Missy, if you don't settle down I'll have to put you out."

"Look, lady, my friends are scared out there. I need to—"

I didn't finish my sentence. She stuck a needle into me. I cried out. She jabbed me really hard! Suddenly, the room began to spin. I flopped back onto the pillow. My memory started to fade. What did I see? Something about Kevin and Devin . . . something really weird happened. What was it?

The nurse smiled at me, "Soon you'll forget all about those Siamese Twins."

Chapter Eleven

I was having the same dream I had before. Anne's body was crushed by the door. The blonde soldier looked into my eyes, making them sting. I cried out and kicked again. I want this to stop. The soldier started to shake me. Suddenly, Kevin and Devin walked into the room. Their arms flailed around as they stumbled to me. The blonde soldier pulled out his gun, and I screamed. I awoke with a shout, "Siamese Twins!" I panted and looked around. James gave me a puzzled look. He sat on the ground next to my bed. He had another tray of food. It looked like breakfast; burnt toast and water. He sighed and shook his head, "You really need to stop getting those morphine injections. You're like a magnet to trouble."

I breathed slowly and said, "I know. The morphine is giving me bad dreams too. James, have you seen Devin and Kevin?"

He shook his head, "No. They weren't at breakfast today. Jenna, you were right about Kristen. Nurse Agnes saw her in the pool last night completely naked with the other kids. The doctors made them stay in the pool. It was snowing outside. None of them made it."

I exclaimed, "That's terrible!"

He nodded, "It had to have been below freezing last night. She said the doctors were in parkas and warm boots. The kids had no clothes; they were stark naked in the deep water. They had to swim to keep afloat, but since they didn't know how to swim they had trouble doing that."

I ate my breakfast. We trained for a little while, but both of our hearts weren't in it. James was thinking about Jacob. He kept talking about all the things they did together before they came here. It was nice, and I tried to listen, but I was really thinking about Devin and Kevin.

Are they still alive? I couldn't believe Dr. Vinkleman pulled off Siamese Twins. How long will they live? Will we be able to see them? Will they be kept in a secret room?

I flopped onto my bed. James sat next to me. I looked over at him. He had no idea what was going on with Kevin and Devin. What would he think? Would he want to leave? He smiled at me, "You're doing great! You stood all by yourself, and you even walked a little. Now we need to focus on lifting your legs up when you walk."

I had to tell him about the Siamese Twins, "James, I saw twins today."

He laughed, "You're funny, Jenna! Ha-ha!"

I shook my head, "Siamese Twins."

He frowned, "I don't get it, what are those?"

I explained, "They are twins that are completely joined together. I tried to walk to your room yesterday. I was doing really great, but I couldn't move my knees. I was shuffling along. I decided to visit Devin and Kevin to show them my progress. I heard them moaning and crying in their room so I opened their door and they . . . they were joined together."

His face went pale. He covered his eyes with his hands. I heard him sniffling. I crawled over to him and wrapped my arms around him. He hugged me tightly, "Oh, Jenna, you're being truthful right?"

I nodded, "I don't lie. The nurse caught me and that's why I was injected with morphine again."

He cried into my bony shoulder. I rubbed his back and tried to quiet his cries. I remember doing this to Anne when she came home crying because the boys were making fun of her. I would sometimes sing to her, but no song came to me now. I broke down and cried too.

Nurse Agnes entered. She saw us hugging and crying. She raised an eyebrow. I let go of James and scooted away from him. He got up and left quickly. She made me walk around and tested my reflexes. She rapped a hammer on my knee. It kicked quickly. She recorded the information in my file. She smiled, "Your progress is getting better. Maybe you'll be able to walk by the end of the week. Quite the miracle."

I said, "James told me about Kristen."

The smile disappeared from her face, "He did? Oh sorry, I was going to tell you."

She sighed and got up to leave. I said quickly, "I saw Kevin and Devin yesterday."

She froze, "Did you now?"

I nodded and replied, "They were joined together. I saw them. Nurse Agnes, what is that doctor doing to them?"

She sat back down on my bed, "Do you remember a different doctor talking to you? He might've been the one that selected you."

I racked my brain for a memory. I answered, "Oh, was it Dr. Keptin?"

She nodded, "He helps out with selection, and he's also a surgeon. He's the one who selected Devin and Kevin for the operation. He also performed the operation. Dr. Vinkleman only supervised."

Now, I hate two doctors: Keptin and Vinkleman. I asked, "Do you think Kevin and Devin will make it?"

She bit her lip. She answered, "I'm not sure. This morning they were having trouble eating, and they are also struggling to use the bathroom."

We were silent. I didn't have any more questions to ask. She got up and left. I immediately jumped up and practiced walking. I definitely want out of this place. I don't care if I get captured and put in the camp. I need to get out of here. In order to do that, I need to be able to walk properly and at least run a little.

My knees felt like they were made of jelly. My feet and toes are working well, and they want to move. However, my knees won't cooperate. I go knock-kneed every time I try to walk properly. I have to keep them apart and use every bit of strength to keep them there.

I practiced for an hour or so and decided to rest for a while. I lied down in bed and closed my eyes. I heard someone shouting in the hall. It could be a patient resisting a shot; I hear it a lot.

My door suddenly banged open, and I jumped in surprise. Kelly stumbled to the floor bawling. She was clutching her eyes and screaming in pain. I was able to spring out of bed and quickly crawl to her. I grabbed her and forced her to look at me. The problem was she couldn't see. She blindly touched my ears and face, twisting her head around.

"Jenna! Oh is that you? Jenna, my eyes! I can't see!" She cried hoarsely. "Dr. Vinkleman gave me eye drops. I remember it! I do! I want to just scratch them out!"

Her blue eyes were inflamed. They were puffy and red. The tear ducts were crusty and red. She kept trying to claw her eyes out. I gripped her hands tightly, "Kelly, how do you remember that? Didn't they give you a shot?"

She tried to twist her hands away from me, but I held a firm grip. She whispered, "The nurses didn't give me enough. I was awake the whole time. It feels like acid is in my eyes! Make it stop!"

I helped her to my bed. She kept crying and trying to scratch her eyes. I scolded, "Stop it! Quit trying to claw your eyes out! I can get help."

She whined, "But it'll stop hurting if I do! I want it to stop, just let me do it! Let me relieve the pain! Don't get help, Jenna, just stay with me! I don't want to die alone."

I kept my vice grip on her hands, "No! You're not going to die alone.

What about Kristen?"

I immediately bit my tongue. She doesn't know about her yet. Suddenly, she laughed, "I know Kristen is dead, and I'm about to join her."

She pulled away from me with such force, I let go. She fell onto the floor and scratched her eyes. I saw blood trickle onto the floor. I couldn't stop her though. I crawled backwards to my bed, watching in horror.

She flipped around and rolled in her own blood. She kept scratching her eyes. I saw something white pop onto the floor. Kelly shrieked and began to pound the ground trying to find it. She splashed around in her blood. The white ball rolled over. A blue eye gazed up at me.

I felt nauseated. Kelly grabbed the ball and gasped violently. She gazed at me with her other eye. I saw her empty socket. It reminded me of Samantha and Alice's hollow sockets.

She grinned from ear to ear, "I'll see Kristen in a bit. Goodbye, Jenna."

She flopped back into her pool of blood. She had a peaceful look on her face. The ceiling began to sink in, and the room started to spin as I fainted.

I woke up to see Nurse Agnes carrying Kelly out. James was there too. A nurse came with Dr. Vinkleman. I screamed and tried to jump out of the bed. She held me down, and Dr. Vinkleman injected me with something. Another nurse escorted James out of my room. He had a worried look in his eyes. I felt the medicine take its toll. My head flopped back onto my pillow.

Chapter Twelve

When I woke up, I was still in my room. I peered over the bed. Kelly's body and blood were gone. I heard a knock at my door. I quietly croaked, "Come in."

James came in with a tray, "Not that I don't like bringing you your food, but this is getting tiring seeing you faint and get shots and stuff. How are you feeling?"

He set the tray next to me. I smiled weakly, "Better. D-did you s-s-see Kelly?"

He nodded, "I came in to take you to the cafeteria for lunch. You were passed out by the bed, and Kelly was dead lying on the floor with her eyeball in her hand. It didn't smell that great either. I went and got Nurse Agnes and then you woke up. It was total pandemonium trying to get you to calm down. I was so worried about you; the fear in your eyes was unbelievable. I wanted to help you, but one of the nurses made me leave."

I eyed the tray. It had a small portion of eggs. As badly cooked as they were, I was so hungry. My stomach let out a grumble. James laughed, "You haven't had much to eat. You slept through lunch and dinner yesterday. You should eat the eggs now."

He handed me the tray. I took it and ate ravenously. The food settled in my stomach. I didn't realize how hungry I was. My stomach felt cramped even thought I ate very little. I guess my stomach has shrunken up. James said, "I've been thinking a lot lately, and I really think we should leave now before anything bad happens to either of us. They want both of our eyes, and they also want to shave your head. They've been targeting our friends lately, and I think we might be next."

I set the tray on the floor. I wanted out of here so bad. I want to just grab James and run out, but I knew that it wouldn't be easy. Also, trying to escape out of the camp will be tricky too. I said, "I want to leave now too. Do you have a plan?"

He nodded, "I think I know a way, but we'd have to leave right now."

"Now?"

He nodded, "There is a truck parked outside of the building right now. I heard the soldiers are going to town this weekend. If we sneak into the truck somehow, we can hitch a ride with them to town. We could start a new life there."

I shook my head, "As nice as your plan sounds, there are a few flaws. Are you sure that some soldiers won't sit in the back?"

"I'm positive. I've seen them drive out, and they never sit in the back. That is where all their cargo is. We can hide under the bags and then jump out before we get to town."

"Ok, wouldn't it seem suspicious for the nurses to see us running around again?" I asked. "They'll inject both of us with morphine on the spot!"

"I've arranged with Nurse Agnes to hide us under a cart. She wants to help us too. She even has some normal clothes for us. We have to meet her in the stairwell right now."

I had a qualm about his plan. It was so risky and if we were to get caught . . . the penalties are simple: torture or death. He saw the uncertainty on my face. He took my hand, "Jenna, it's now or never. I promise I'll protect you."

"Promise?"

He nodded, "I promise."

We stood up, and my legs wobbled slightly. I could feel them wanting to give in. This won't work. I sat back down with a sigh, "My legs still won't work. They just aren't strong enough."

He picked me up like a baby. He smiled, "I can carry you. You're not heavy at all. I don't mind."

I blushed. I said softly, "You can put me down now. I can walk, but not run."

"Oh right sorry," he slowly put me down. "You ready to do this?"

"I just can't believe how sudden it is."

"Aw don't tell me you've become attached to this place," he chuckled.

I laughed, "Definitely not that."

"Well what are we waiting for?" he asked. We walked out the door together holding hands. So far, I was doing pretty well. We kept a steady pace. I saw Mallory at the end of the hall. I heard James mutter under his breath. "Great. Mad Mallory is here."

She slightly cocked her head and smiled. She really was creepy, "Going somewhere?"

I opened my mouth, but James elbowed me in the stomach. He snapped, "None of your business. Go away, Mallory."

We ran down the stairs. I heard her little voice call, "Shame to hear about your brother!"

He stopped and glared up at her. She stood at the top of the stairs and grinned down at us. He snarled, "What do you know about him?"

She laughed, "I know he didn't make it through the . . . eye surgery."

I felt James grab my hand and squeeze it hard. I felt my bones popping. They glared at each other. She took a step down and he barked, "Stay up there, Mallory! Don't follow us."

She smirked, "If I don't, the nurses will!"

I whispered, "She's getting into your head. Let's go find Nurse Agnes."

He nodded and led me further down the stairs. I heard her voice call out, "You should've listened to her, James! Jacob probably would've survived!"

I saw James flinch. I squeezed his hand gently. I knew he was mad that he didn't listen to me. He knew that if he had believed me in the first place, his brother would still be alive. I felt so sorry for him. I probably wouldn't have trusted me if I were him. I was so frantic and weird I probably made Mallory seem normal. I understand why he didn't trust me, but now he's beating himself up for it.

Nurse Agnes stood at the bottom of the stairs. She had the cart with her too. She seemed distracted, looking side to side to make sure no one could see us. She whispered, "Did anyone see you?"

I answered, "Mallory saw us. I think she might tell a nurse."

She nodded, "I think I could get you out of here faster than that girl can get a nurse to believe something. She's an odd one; most of the nurses don't trust her."

James grumbled, "No one does."

Nurse Agnes handed us our clothes. I got a dark, grey dress, stockings, black boots, gloves, a scarf, and wool coat. James got a pair of trousers, a blue sweater, long socks, boots, a wool coat, gloves, and a cap. She shielded me as I dressed. I looked over at James. He already had his clothes on and was tying his shoes. I hope this will be enough to keep us warm; especially since we are going to be in the back of a truck exposed to the elements.

I straightened my clothes. They looked like something I would wear back at home. I smiled at Nurse Agnes, "Thank you for helping us. We couldn't have survived here without you."

She nodded, "Your welcome. I'm just happy I could finally help someone."

She pushed us under the cart. She threw a cloak over it. We squatted under the cart. My knees were killing me, and I kept falling backwards into

James. He almost fell out of the cart. He wrapped an arm around me to keep me steady. I felt the heat rise into my cheeks.

The cart slowly stopped. He whispered, "Nurse Agnes will tell me when no one is around. I'll help you out and carry you to the truck."

"Ok," I whispered back. I heard Nurse Agnes's heels clicking. She's checking the area. I heard her click back to the cart. I heard her mumble something, and then James jumped out. I was still cramped inside the cart. He pulled me out and carried me to the door. I looked back to see Nurse Agnes running away with the cart.

He pushed the doors open. The frigid winter air filled my lungs. I felt a cough coming up and tried to hold it in. I swallowed franticly trying to wet my throat until the feeling went away.

We were on a mad 100 yard dash to the truck. First place gets you a new life. Anything slower . . . well I'm just going to keep winning in my mind. We made it to the truck without anyone seeing us. James boosted me up, and I climbed into the bed of the truck. I turned around and helped pull him into the truck. There were blankets, pillows, and bags scattered in the bed. I hid under several of the blankets and tossed a couple of bags and pillows over myself for warmth.

James crawled right next to me. We both piled blankets on top of us. We huddled together in the bed. Even though we were wearing warm clothes, the cool air swept underneath the clothes and blankets and bit into our skin. I was shaking so hard I rattled the truck. James tried his best to warm me, but he was freezing cold too.

He whispered, "Where are the soldiers? They aren't even here!"

I chattered my teeth, trying to form words, "I d-d-d-d-don't kn-kn-kn-know."

He rubbed my arms, "You're so cold. I'm sorry. I didn't think it would be this cold in the afternoon. I've forgotten what it was like being outside."

Suddenly, we heard voices. They were laughing and talking in German. I looked at James. He mouthed, "Soldiers."

I heard them all pile into the truck. The bed shook, moving our bodies around. I felt the truck's engine rumble to life. The truck slowly pressed forward. I smiled at James. He smiled back. We are escaping. We made it!

The truck drove through the camp. I really wanted to see if I could spot Emma or Mother. I knew I wouldn't be able to rescue them, but I wanted them to know I'm ok. I tried to poke my head out, but James stopped me, "No! If anyone sees us they'll point us out."

I hissed, "I want to find my sister Emma. I need to see her and Mother one last time."

He nodded. I poked my head out of the blankets. I can't fully explain what I saw. There are too many words that go with too many faces. There was so much pain and sorrow. Peoples' bodies were nothing but skin and bones. Their bald heads were scratched and bruised, and their eyes were dull and lifeless. Bodies were strewn all over the ground. I saw an old man beat a little girl for her piece of bread. He pushed her to the ground and snatched her bread.

I felt James's face next to me. I turned to look at him. He had tears in his eyes. He whispered, "There she is, my mama."

I looked to where he was staring. A tall woman and an elderly woman walked by the barracks. The tall woman had a dull, bald head. She wore a baggy, striped uniform. She looked in our direction. Her face is very beautiful; with high cheekbones and big, green eyes.

She smiled widely. James gasped, "She sees me."

Her smile quickly faded as a soldier approached her. He pushed her down and took the old woman. I could feel James want to jump out and help his mama. I squeezed his hand gently. He looked at me and climbed down, "At least she knows I'm alive and ok."

I tried to find Mother and Emma. I didn't want to get too hopeful. They could be working or in a barrack sleeping, or dead. Suddenly, I saw Emma. Her long mane was gone. It's weird seeing her with a bald head. She was also much thinner. She was still beautiful though. Another woman walked with her. Emma held the woman's hand and talked to her gently. Emma smiled slightly, and the woman had a permanent frown on her face. I recognized that frown. It was the same frown I got when I stayed out too late, or when I got a bad grade on a test. I realized that woman was my mother.

Emma looked at the truck, then directly at me. She gasped and pulled on Mother's sleeve. Mother looked at me. Her frown disappeared from her face. A bright smile replaced it. I smiled back. Tears streamed down Mother's face as she grinned at me. Emma smiled and nodded at me. I nodded back and slid back under the blankets.

James wrapped his arm around me, "I hope our families get out."

"I hope that they get out too."

Chapter Thirteen

I wanted to fall asleep in the truck. I was so tired, and I wanted to rest my eyes for a bit. A few things prevented me from doing that: 1) James wouldn't stop flopping into me. He couldn't help it; the truck shook a lot, especially when we went over bumps. I am in the corner of the bed, and when he flops into me, I bang my head on the side. I tried to use a pillow to cover my head, but it still hurt every time I hit it. 2) I thought I was cold before the truck was moving, but now it's moving, and the cold air whips my skin. I'm hiding underneath three blankets, and I can still feel the air's cold sting. 3) James wants me to be alert and awake in case we have to leave quickly. He says that the soldiers might stop to smoke or get something from the back. We have to be ready to hide the best we can, or try to run.

I felt something wet on the blankets. I poked my head out slightly. It was snowing. I huddled back next to James. He looked at me and smiled. He whispered, "You have snowflakes on your eyelashes."

I blinked. I felt the wet snow melt on my eyelashes. He mumbled, "Wow."

"What?" I asked.

He smiled sheepishly, "The way the snow looks on your eyes; you look angelic."

My cheeks heated up so much that all the snowflakes melted off my face. I smiled and looked away. What was I supposed to say to that?

The truck stopped abruptly. James and I banged heads. We tried not to groan too loud. The truck's wheels were spinning, but the truck wouldn't move. The engine groaned and finally turned off.

I heard the passengers jump out and talk. New voices joined them. I poked my head up to see what was going on. James yanked me down and hissed, "No! They might see you. Wait for a minute."

I nodded and sank down. I felt my heart thump harder. I couldn't hear anything else besides that steady beat. I felt my throat tighten. I wanted to clear it, but I didn't want the soldiers to hear me. James looked alert. He was listening to them talking. I heard their voices slowly fade away.

James carefully pulled the blankets off. He looked around quickly. No one was there. He stumbled off the truck. I grabbed a blanket and followed him. He smiled, "Good thinking, we'll need that. Let's go!"

He picked me up and turned in circles trying to decide where to go. I listened for sounds of civilization. Suddenly, I heard loud voices. The soldiers! "James, they're coming back!"

James panicked and dropped me. I cried out, immediately slapping my mouth shut. I twisted my head around. I saw the soldiers coming through a woody area. They were carrying guns. I looked frantically at James. He was frozen with fear. I stood up, "We need to run! Let's go!"

I ran as fast as I could to a ditch on the other side of the truck. I hissed at him, "What are you doing? Get over here!"

He looked like he was about to jump to me and land safely behind the truck in the ditch out of harm's way. All we would have to do is run to a village and start a new life just like he said. All of it changed with a loud gunshot.

It all happened so fast. His arms reached out for me. His eyes were focused on me, and then suddenly he fell on his side. He let out a horrible shriek. I saw blood shoot from his chest and mouth. My ears started ringing. It took everything I had inside me not to scream. I bit my lip, held my ringing ears and tried to scream silently in my head.

I heard a soldier laugh through the screams in my head. It was a menacing, evil laugh. I don't understand how someone can laugh at a person dying. How one can watch death with such sadistic pleasure.

I thought that they might be able to see me, so I covered my body up with snow. I heard them talk a little longer and then get in their truck and drive off. I pushed my snow layers off and crawled to James. He had two bullet holes in his chest. Blood trickled down his lips. I choked out tears. He turned his head slightly to me. I let out a quiet wail. He smiled and slowly touched my face, "I'm . . . fine."

I cried, "Don't you dare leave me, James. I can't do this without you. James, don't die! Oh please don't leave me, don't die please!"

"I want . . . you to know I . . . thought you were so pretty . . . ever since I met . . . you. I will always . . . treasure you in my . . . heart," he gasped.

I felt my heart break. I shook my head, "No! Don't say this stuff! I can save you!"

I wrapped the blanket around his bloody wound. I put some pressure on it. He groaned loud and clenched my arm, "No, stop . . . I want this."

I sniffled, "No you will live! You can't die!"

He moaned and released his grip on my arm. I focused on the wound. Blood seeped through the wool blanket; it felt warm against my hands. I couldn't stop the bleeding. I needed to get him help. When I looked back at him, his eyes were closed. I felt his chest, and I couldn't feel him breathing. I checked his pulse, but I couldn't find it.

I pulled him closer to me. I cradled his cold body in my arms. I held his face close to mind and kissed his forehead. That was the first time I'd ever kissed a boy and a dead one at that. I should've kissed him while he was alive. I cried and hugged him closer to me.

I had to bury him. I looked around. The ground was covered in snow. My hands were already freezing and shaking. I pulled him towards the ditch. I laid him in the snow. Hopefully the snowfall will bury him. I said a quiet prayer for him and then fled the opposite direction that the soldiers went.

I tripped over logs and dodged tree branches. I wrapped the blanket around my shoulders, but I was still freezing cold. I could barely keep a steady jog without wobbling and flapping my arms. James was still on my mind. His cold, dead face reappears and haunts my mind.

I fell over a log. I stifled a cry and rolled up into a ball. This wasn't as easy as he said it would be. He made it sound like starting a new life would be so easy. I can barely even get out of the woods to civilization!

I can't do this without him. It's impossible! I can't run or stay on my feet for a long period of time. I should've stayed at the hospital, at least it was warm there and there was some food. Maybe I should go back.

No, no, no what am I thinking? It was horrible there! All my friends died, and I could barely eat because of all the morphine they gave me. I was sick all the time, and the only thing that was keeping me alive was James. I can't go back. I won't go back. James would want me to continue.

I hobbled on through the snow. There has to be a village not too far from here right? I shivered and wrapped the damp blanket tighter around my shoulders.

Suddenly, a gust of wind knocked me over. I landed on a log that was split in two. The splintered wood cut through my clothes and scratched my skin. I cried out in pain. I tried to stand up, but my right ankle was caught between the split log, and I fell again.

Agonizing pain shot through my right ankle. It felt like someone had amputated it. I couldn't help but to scream. I pulled up my skirt and examined my ankle; It had already begun to swell. I think I only sprained it, but it hurt so much.

Anne always had injuries from playing sports. Because of all her injuries, I was used to wrapping up a sprained ankle, or putting ice on a sore muscle. However, out here in the middle of nowhere, I didn't have anything. I didn't know what to do.

I slowly stood up and put a little bit of pressure on my right foot, but I almost collapsed. The pain was excruciating! I grabbed a strong branch and used it to help balance myself. I can't walk with my leg like this. My toes are still numb, and I'm not sure if it is from the shots or the snow.

I need something to help me walk. A walking stick! I tugged on a dead branch, but I was so weak and tired I could barely bend it! I pulled my body up on it. Even using all my weight the branch barely lowered. I jiggled it up and down trying to get it to snap. Finally, after a few minutes of pulling and jiggling, I got the branch to snap. I fell flat on my butt. It was better to land on my butt than my legs. I used the stick to help myself up. I tried balancing on it, and it worked perfectly! It was just the right height for me! I continued walking.

The snow cascaded down from the sky. It glittered on the ground making it look like I was walking on white diamonds. Soon the snow became less beautiful and more annoying. The snow piled up in huge drifts, making it almost impossible to move. I felt like I was swimming in a sea of white, fluffy clouds! The best thing about my walking stick was that it doubled as a ruler! I could measure how deep a snow drift was in front of me. It helped prevent me from getting stuck in a huge snow drift.

Whenever I was thirsty, I scooped up a pile of snow and let it melt in my mouth. It was freezing cold, and it seemed like I could never get enough water. My stomach groaned and protested. I wish I had thought of bringing food with me. The wind began to pick up as nighttime came. I've been traveling nonstop all day, and I haven't found any signs of civilization. I haven't even heard any soldiers or vehicles! Was this the middle of nowhere?

I had to stop. My left foot ached so much from holding most of my weight up, and my right foot hurt just as much. I needed to find a way to treat my ankle.

A howl broke the silence of the night, and a chorus of howls followed. A wolf pack was nearby. I had to get to safety or I'd be their dinner. Speaking of dinner, I was unbelievably hungry. In fact, my stomach was howling along with the wolves!

The only place I could think of to hide and be safe from the wolves was high up in a tree. I picked a tree with lots of strong, sturdy looking branches. I set my walking stick on the ground. I tied my blanket around my shoulders and hopped up to the first branch pulling myself up. I don't want to be too high up, just high enough so the wolves can't get me. I climbed up another branch. I was careful not to put full pressure on my right foot. I finally settled on the fourth branch. I was very high off the ground, and the branch was thick and strong enough for me to sit on.

I untied the blanket and laid it on my body. I tried to relax, but I couldn't. The cold chill of the air was relentless, and the howls of the wolves kept me alert. Slowly, I felt my eyes droop. I heard more howls echo through the night as I drifted off to sleep, dreaming of James.

I felt the bright sun shining on my face. I groaned and rubbed my eyes. The sun's light reflected off the white ground, making it very hard to see. After I let my eyes adjust for a minute, I shook the snow off my blanket.

As I prepared to climb down, I noticed that the ground looked closer than it did yesterday. I realized it had snowed all night. There must be at least five more feet of snow on the ground!

I carefully climbed down to the last branch. I was a little scared to jump down. I could get stuck inside a big snow drift and never come out! I pushed the fear aside and jumped. I fell into the cold, white pillow of snow. I sat up and pushed my way out of my snow jail.

I searched for my walking stick. I'm sure I left it at the base of the tree, but I couldn't find it! I dug through the snow, but I couldn't even find the ground! My hands quickly became numb, and I gave up on my search. I'll just look for another branch to snap off. Unfortunately, there were no branches within my reach. I'll have to walk without one.

After hobbling at least four miles without a walking stick, I became completely exhausted. The only thing I've eaten is snow. I have to rest about every 30 minutes because I tire out so fast from lack of food. My shoes are soaked, and my toes were numb. My clothes are wet from tripping into snow drifts, and my blanket has no purpose anymore. This was turning into a nightmare. I thought the point of leaving the hospital was to run away from my nightmare and escape into my perfect dream.

Every time I feel like I'm ready to give up and die, I hear trucks, or people talking. I sometimes smell smoke or food. I think this might be in my imagination, but it keeps me moving forward.

I finally had to rest. My ankle had swollen up twice its size. I have no clue how far I've walked, and all I know is that I'm too tired to carry on anymore. I stumbled to the nearest tree and fell asleep shivering against it.

Suddenly, I felt someone shake me, "Jenna, wake up!"

I opened my eyes. James was floating in front of me. He smiled and laughed, "C'mon, Jacob!"

Jacob appeared next to him. Both of them hovered inches above the ground. They laughed and took my hands. James smiled at me, "You're doing great, Jenna. Keep going strong!"

I gasped, "James! It's you! Oh, James, I miss you so much!"

"I miss you too," he replied. He squeezed my hands gently. His touch felt so warm and real.

"I miss you too!" Jacob mocked, "I'm doing great too, Jenna. Thanks for your concern."

I chuckled, "I miss you too, Jacob."

He blushed. James squeezed my hand. It felt so warm and real. He smiled, "I know it's been hard for you, but you've been doing great without me. I'm so proud of you."

"Please come back!" I begged. "I'm not doing great at all. I need you, guys!"

He shook his head solemnly, "I can't do that, Jenna. You have to do this alone. I'm sorry."

They lowered me to the ground. I pouted, "This isn't fair! I'm supposed to do this with you! We were a team! I'm so scared, James, I need you."

He looked around as if he was searching for someone, "I'm sorry, Jenna, but we have to go!"

"James, please don't go! Jacob!" I shouted. "Don't leave me! I can't do this alone! Come back!"

"Goodbye, Jenna!" the twins called. "You can do this!"

I woke up gasping. I glanced around the woods. No one was here. I was alone. I buried my face into my hands and cried. I felt more alone than I had ever felt in my life. That dream felt so real. I remember the heat of James's hand and how he squeezed it tightly. I remember Jacob's laugh. It was like they were right there with me. Was it really a dream?

I stood up slowly and trudged forward. While I was walking up the hill, James's words echoed in my mind. *You're doing great, Jenna! I miss you so much! I'm so proud of you.*

Did he really say that? He was so real. No, James is dead. I'm imagining things. The lack of food was getting to my head and making me see things. It was just a dream.

After I finally got to the top of the hill, I checked out the view. I saw a small church steeple not too far away! It was past a few miles of forest in a small clearing. I bet there's a village there! I jumped up excitedly, but came crashing down hard and fast.

I had landed on my ankle, making it collapse. I tumbled down the hill. I bumped into logs and rocks concealed by the snow. I finally stopped tumbling. I looked up at the hill and saw a trail of blood following the path I had made. I examined my arms and legs. My clothes were cut up by the obstacles. Scratches and deep cuts covered my legs and arms.

I slowly stood up and moaned in pain. My whole body was an aching bruise! I took a step forward and gasped sharply. I knew I couldn't walk anymore; I just couldn't. I fell to the ground and crawled. I saw blood dripping to the ground. I wiped my nose and checked my hand. My nose was bleeding. I groaned and crawled through the snow.

Crawling was worse than walking. My body was becoming colder because I was pressed against the snow. My clothes were absolutely soaked. I had to practically swim through snow drifts, but at least the chilly breeze didn't hit me as badly.

It became darker and colder. I couldn't crawl anymore. I was so exhausted, but I couldn't rest. The wolves were howling again, and they were louder and closer than last time.

I wish I could climb another tree, but I couldn't stand or walk. I had nowhere to go. The howls were getting louder. I heard snarls and growls and the sound of paws trotting across the snow. I started breathing deeply; my heart was racing so fast I thought it would jump out of my chest.

I saw a shadow rush behind a log. A pair of furry ears poked up behind the log. It was a wolf. He growled softly. That's it, I'm a goner. The wolf jumped over the log and stalked closer to me. Blood stains covered the outside of its mouth. Looks like it already ate its appetizer! Time for the main course. Me!

I cringed and waited for the beast to attack me with its sharp claws and teeth. It never came. As the wolf prepared to pounce, I heard a loud crack and blood spilled out of its left shoulder. It howled in pain and stumbled away. I heard the retreat of its pack too.

I heard footsteps crunching through the snow behind me. It couldn't be another wolf; it sounded too big. I used my last bit of strength to flip over to see who it was. It was a man. He bent over and gently picked me up and carried me away, not saying a word. I felt faint and passed out.

Chapter Fourteen

I woke up in a warm bed, and it felt amazing. I had forgotten what a warm bed even felt like. The warm sheets and blankets engulfed me in heat. I sat up slowly. I was wearing a long shirt that went down to my knees. I lifted the shirt up. My waist and arms and legs were bandaged. I was still wearing my bra and underwear Nurse Agnes had given me. Did the man undress me?

A woman walked into the room. She had blonde hair that was in a short braid. Her skin was dull, and her clothes looked worn out. She wore an apron with many patches on it. Her eyes were a bright, light blue. She smiled widely showing her sparkling, white teeth. Her eyes and smile seemed to brighten up her whole appearance, making her look younger.

I lowered my shirt. She read my mind and chuckled, "Don't worry, dear, I undressed you not my husband."

I smiled a little. She walked over to me and checked my bandages. She handed me a glass of water. I drank it quickly. She asked, "What is your name?"

I answered, "Jenna." I didn't want to give her my last name, Altsman.

She smiled, "That's a pretty name. What were you doing in the woods so late?"

I froze. Should I tell her the truth? Well, my friend and I escaped from this concentration camp, and he died saving me. I got lost in the woods trying to find somewhere safe to hide out, and do you know you could be arrested for keeping me here?

Maybe I'll tell her half the truth, "I got lost in the woods." That was more like a fourth of the truth.

She sighed, "Well if my husband wasn't out hunting, you could've died out there. You should be more careful, Jenna."

I nodded, "Thank you for helping me."

"You're welcome. Now we need to tell your parents where you are. We have a telephone you can use to call them."

I had to come up with a lie fast, "We don't have a telephone."

She looked at me strangely, "Do you not live in the village? Most people here have telephones."

"Uh no we live in the woods. My father likes it that way."
She raised an eyebrow, "Well how are you getting home?"

"Now that the blizzard is over I can make my way home."

Her eyebrow was still raised, "My husband will help you. I can't just let you run out in the woods alone. Your wounds are healed up well enough so you can leave now if you like."

I wish I could stay with them and just say I don't have any family. I could say I'm an orphan, and I want to stay with them. I looked around the room. I saw a small picture on the nightstand and examined it. Two blonde girls hugged each other and smiled at the camera. They were identical. I gasped and dropped it.

The woman asked, "Is there something wrong?"

"Who are these girls?" I asked.

The woman's face changed when she saw the picture. The doubtful look she has been giving me was replaced with a small, sad smile. She sighed wistfully, "Those are my adopted daughters, Kelly and Kristen. I have two daughters named Kaitlynn and Kristina. Kelly and Kristen's parents were sent to a concentration camp, and I took care of them. We were close friends with her family, and the girls got along wonderfully. One day, the soldiers came for Kelly and Kristen. Kaitlynn and Kristina couldn't bear to see them go. They had caused such a scene. One of the soldiers said the girls could be useful to them because they were twins, and they would take them too. I felt like I had died that day."

I wonder if I should tell her. I think she should know. If she's ok with Kelly and Kristen being Jewish, then she should be ok with me. She has to know. "I knew Kelly and Kristen," I said tentatively.

She smiled, "Oh, were you friends with them?"

I shook my head, "No. You see . . . I'm not who you think I am. I'm a Jew. I went to the same concentration camp as them. I'm sorry, but none of them made it. I escaped with a friend. He died saving me. I got lost in the woods. I'm so sorry about your daughters."

She was silent. She had a shocked look on her face. Now I regret telling her everything. She finally spoke, "So . . . you say you're a Jew?"

I nodded. She bit her lip in thought. She asked, "Where were you going to go?"

I shrugged my shoulders, "I don't know."

She asked, "Would you like to stay with us?"

I shook my head, "No! You could get arrested if soldiers find out you're hiding me."

"I can't just send you out there!"

"I don't want you to get hurt," I begged. I couldn't believe I was giving up a warm bed, a roof over my head, and nice people who were willing to take care of me. However, I knew if anything happened to them because of me I couldn't live with myself. James has already died for me, and I can't let anyone else die for me again. "The soldiers kill people who hide Jews. If you could take me to the next village, I would appreciate it very much."

"The next village is full of soldiers. It is where they go when they have time off. I'm sorry dear, but you have to stay with us."

"You don't know how much I'd love that, but I can't!" I insisted. "The soldiers are ruthless! You should know that! They took your daughters away! They'll take me away and kill me, you, and your husband too!"

The woman frowned. She got up and left my room. A burly man entered the room. He said in a low, husky voice, "Hello, Jenna."

It was her husband; the man that saved me. I smiled, "Hello. Thank you for saving me and taking care of me."

He replied, "You're welcome. My wife and I miss having a child in our house. We would love for you to stay."

I shook my head, "Believe me I'd love to stay, but I can't. If the soldiers find out a Jew is living with you—"

He interrupted me, "My wife and I understand the consequences, Jenna, but we can't just let you run off. You have a better chance of living here than on the run out there."

I asked, "How? I have blonde hair and blue eyes. If I don't say I'm a Jew, then people won't even notice me! You didn't even know until I told you! I can easily blend in!"

He interrupted me again, "Kelly and Kristen said the same thing! After the soldiers took their parents, they never said a word about their faith! They tried their best to blend in and keep to themselves! The soldiers still found them, and then they took my daughters too! My beautiful girls are now dead! I don't want you to die either."

I said quietly, "I'm not your daughter though. Let me go."

"You don't understand. A young girl can't live by herself! You're too weak, and you can't survive on your own. Please just stay with us, and we will take care of you."

"I'm not weak!" I yelled. "I've been through so much you don't even underst…"

"Hush!" he bellowed.

I was getting tired of him interrupting me. I shouted, "No! You don't understand! Do you know what I've been through? Do you know what I've seen? Compared to me you're the weak one!"

He glowered at me. I lowered my voice, "Thank you for taking care of me, but I must go."

He lowered his voice too, "You are a weak, helpless girl, and you will not leave."

He walked out the door and slammed it behind him. I jumped out of the bed and ran to the door. My sides began to ache, but I tried to ignore the pain. I jiggled the doorknob but it wouldn't move. I yelled, "Let me out!"

I couldn't believe it. I'm locked up again. I kicked the door. I heard the man yell, "Stop!"

I am not staying here. There's got to be some way out. I looked around the room. There was a small vanity, a bed, a nightstand, a wardrobe and an oak chest. A small window was beside the bed. Maybe I could squeeze through it.

I awkwardly walked to the wardrobe and opened it up. Girl clothes were messily stashed inside the drawers. I slowly put on a purple dress and black stockings. I found a white coat that will help me blend in with the snow. I looked under the bed and found a few pairs of shoes. I tried them all on, but they were too big. I put on a couple pairs of socks and tried on a pair of boots. They fit much better.

I pushed the chest in front of the window. I climbed onto it and tried to open the window. It slid open halfway. I tried to push it higher, but it wouldn't budge. Now I really had to squeeze through. I took off my coat and tossed it outside. I heard footsteps outside my door. I had to hurry; I pulled myself through the window. My upper torso went through. The cold air hit my face, and I almost squealed. I grunted trying to get my lower half through.

Suddenly, I heard the door slam open. I heard the man yell my name. I pushed harder, and I felt myself slide out the window. The man grabbed my right leg. I screamed in pain as he squeezed my bad ankle. I desperately tried to kick with my left leg. He yanked on my right leg, jerking it around. I thought my sides were going to explode. All the blood was rushing to my face, and it was getting harder to breathe. I felt my left leg collide with something. I heard a husky scream as I dropped into the snow.

I heard him yell, "You don't know what you're doing! You'll never survive on your own! You're making a big mistake, Jenna!"

I grabbed the coat and never looked back.

Chapter Fifteen

After running for about a mile, I stopped to rest. My sides felt like they're going to split open, and my head and ankle felt the same way. The man's words echoed in my head:

> *"You're a weak, helpless girl." "You don't know what you're doing!" "You're making a big mistake, Jenna!"*

Should I go back? I thought about the warm bed I had slept in, and all the clothes in the wardrobe I could have worn. The home cooked meals I could have eaten and hot baths I could have taken.

Are all those things worth risking someone's safety? The man definitely seemed like he would be very possessive of me, and I am not weak or helpless! I battled a polio virus! I'm sure if I would have stayed he wouldn't let me out of that bedroom. I would have been a prisoner in that house. I bet he wouldn't like me writing either.

The only person who approved of my writing was Papa. No one else liked that I wrote about serious things like politics or war. Papa thought it was amazing that I thought like that. He even used some of my writings in his column in the newspaper. I didn't mind that he did. He always showed me the printed paper and scribbled out his name and wrote mine there. So it was like I was reading a story that I had actually written in the paper with my name on it!

I felt tears forming in my eyes, thinking of Papa made me miss him more and Anne too. It also made me think about James and Jacob. What if I dreamed about them again? I think that's how I saw them. I sat down and leaned against a tree. I thought hard about them.

There was a tap on my shoulder so I looked up. James! He wore white trousers and a white shirt. His green-apple eyes sparkled. I finally found my voice and said, "Hey."

He chuckled, "Lost for words?"

I nodded, "Yeah."

He smiled, "I've been with you this whole time in your heart. You've put up a struggle to survive without me, Jenna. You're amazing."

"James, I've missed you so much."

He squeezed my shoulder and said, "I miss you too, but I'm with you all the time, Jenna. Don't forget that."

"I won't!"

He nodded and glared around, "I have to go now. Remember, I'm always with you ok? Jacob too!"

"Can I see Jacob too? Where is he? James, don't go!"

He slowly disappeared. I opened my eyes. I had been asleep. The cold silence of the air seemed deafening. I brought my knees up to my chin and cried. I needed James now more than ever. Talking to him made me feel lighter, like all the burdens and pains on my chest were lifted. When he left, they all came crashing back down on me. I wish I could be with him instead of here by myself.

I know he wants me to continue. That's all he's ever wished for was for me to be free and happy. I guess I'll try to make his last wish come true and if not . . . maybe my wish will come true.

I got back on my feet and hobbled on. After walking a few miles, I could smell smoke. I looked up at the sky. The trees blocked my view, but I could definitely smell smoke. It made my eyes water. I followed my nose. The smell became overwhelming.

Finally, I saw a trail of smoke curl and spin in the air. It spiraled around the trees and led me to civilization. I traveled until I found a small village. A few cottages were scattered in the snow. Smoke rose from the chimneys. A distant memory of the red smoke puffing from the crematories came to my mind, but I pushed it away.

I stumbled to the ground. I did it. I did the impossible. I smiled and cried in the snow. My hands clenched the snow until it melted in my hands. I'm done running. Nobody will know who I am here. I was free, but something made me not want to celebrate.

James. Seeing him again brought back a tidal wave of emotion. Why did he have to be a hero? Why did he have to save me? I was nothing but deadweight to him! I never planned anything, or been any help to him. It's my fault he died. Why did he care about me so much? What even made him like me?

I threw a snowball in frustration. We could've died together. It would've saved me a broken heart in the end. I banged on the ground with my fists. I threw snow around and cried. I flopped to the ground and continued crying.

I heard a door shut and looked up. A girl walked out of a cottage. She saw me and ran to me. She started speaking German. I assumed she had asked me what was wrong or if I was ok. I answered weakly, "Help me!"

She nodded and helped me up. She seemed surprised how scrawny I was. I probably weighed as much as a bundle of sticks. The girl looked really strong. She was short and stocky. Her hair was blonde and in an elaborate, braided bun. She wore a white dress with a brown apron.

She took me inside her home. The warmth from the fire hit my skin making it prickle. The warmth spread from my fingers to my toes. The whole cottage smelled like warm apple pie.

She laid me in a bed and tucked me in. I snuggled into the quilted blankets. I wanted to go to sleep right there, but the girl came back with a bowl of soup. The aroma made my mouth water. I remembered that the woman and the man didn't feed me. I can't believe how hungry I was.

She helped me sit up straight. I ate slowly, savoring every spoonful. The soup was chowder. It was creamy and delicious. I scraped my spoon at the bottom of the bowl. I felt disappointed that the heavenly soup was all gone.

The girl came back holding a small plate of pie. My eyes lit up, and I sat up straighter. She smiled and handed it to me. I ate the pie quickly.

I haven't had pie since we left my old house. We used to bake all the time there. We made so many pies we could've opened a bakery! When we moved into the apartment, we barely had enough money to pay rent. We couldn't buy the ingredients needed for the pies, so we stopped baking. It really upset Anne and me. We used to talk and bake pies all day. It is a great memory.

The girl came back and sat at the foot of the bed. She watched me pick up the crumbs from the plate. My stomach rumbled a satisfying sigh. I burped and blushed, "Sorry."

She laughed and said, "It's fine. I'm Heidi Olglen. I noticed you don't speak much German?"

I can't let her know I'm Jewish, but I don't know any other language besides Dutch. I nodded, "Yes I speak Dutch more than I do German. It's easier to me."

She smiled, "Well you are lucky I know enough Dutch to talk to someone. Most people in this village speak German. What is your name?"

Tricky question. Should I lie? I should definitely change my name at least. What's a good German last name? I remembered Papa's boss's last name. I answered, "Clara Steinenhauser."

"Ah a Steinenhauser? There are a few of them here," Heidi rubbed her cheek and nodded. "So what were you doing out in the cold snow? If I hadn't walked outside to retrieve more wood, I would have never seen you."

I looked down at my plate, conjuring a story up in my head. I was very good at making elaborate lies in school on why I was late to class. I usually got away with it. Papa always said I had his creative mind. I said, "I ran away from home. My father is very abusive, and my Mother died when I was five. I have a brother named Erik, but he joined the Nazi Party, and I haven't seen him since. My father was abusing me, so I left a few days ago."

Heidi nodded sympathetically, "I'm really sorry. You can stay with me for a few days if you like. Perhaps you could move into a cottage near here too. It's a very nice village, I think you'd like it here."

I smiled, "You're so kind. Thank you!"

She stood up, "You're welcome. You could get a job down at the tavern. Billy's always looking for new waitresses and bartenders. You could work at the bar with me."

I've never worked with alcoholic drinks. Mother and Papa weren't drinkers. They said it was a waste of money, and it made you sick if you drank too much. I mumbled, "Oh I don't know. I might not stay for long."

Heidi smiled, "I'm not forcing you to, but you could start a new life here far away from your mean father. Just give it some thought."

I flinched. Start a new life; that's what James told me. Heidi walked out of the room, "Goodnight, Jenna!"

I sunk down into the fluffy blankets. This beats that hard cot at the hospital. I never realized how itchy that blanket was there until now. These blankets were warm and soft.

I remembered in the truck how James had draped more blankets onto me. He had whispered, "Don't want you to catch a cold."

I rubbed the blankets. A warm tear fell down my face onto the blanket. I slowly fell asleep and dreamed of James.

Chapter Sixteen

I stayed in bed all day. Heidi brought me loads of food. It really brought my strength up. I completely felt my legs for the first time. I could easily wiggle my toes and bend my knees.

"I'm leaving for my shift at the tavern. I'll be back soon," Heidi said.

I thought about what my next move was; to either leave or stay. A part of me wants to start a new life here. The way Heidi had described the little village made it sound like a perfect haven. I'd like to work at the tavern with her and maybe get a place of my own. However, another part of me would like to keep going. I want to travel the world and write about everything I saw. It's been my dream since I was a little girl.

Sometimes, I think I should forget about James and maybe the pain of losing him would go away. Come to think of it, I don't think I ever will forget him. He believed in me when all hope was lost, and that's something I will never forget. It's something I don't want to forget.

Heidi came back after her shift at the tavern. She was in a good, bubbly mood. I asked Heidi about herself. She told me about her life. She has lived in this little village all of her life. Her parents live a few cottages down from her. She's worked at the tavern since she was 17 years old. She's 23 years old now. I lied and said I was 18 years old.

After dinner, she suggested we take a walk around the village. She made me take a bath because I smelled like a hog. I couldn't smell how bad I was because I was so used to the stench. I haven't bathed for a week.

I took a quick, hot bath. I could've stayed under the warm water forever, but I really wanted to see the village. I almost forgot what shampoo and soap was like. How the shampoo lathered in my hair and how soap left little bubbles on my skin. I forgot what clean hair felt like. I never knew how amazing it was to have a clean body. My hair now smelled like lavender, and my skin smelled like lilacs.

She also let me borrow one of her dresses and a pair of boots. I picked a blue dress because it brought out my eyes and black boots. Heide's boots fit me much better than the oversized ones I had stolen from the couple.

We silently walked through the village. She would break the silence and explain what was inside some of the cottages. She has a very loud voice. She said, "Oh and that's Billy's Tavern. Would you like to meet Billy? Have you decided if you want to stay yet?"

I shook my head no, "I'd rather not go inside the tavern, and I'm not sure if I will be staying here."

She looked down sheepishly, "Oh, well that's fine."

We were quiet for a minute. Suddenly, people stumbled out of the tavern, laughing loudly and smoking cigarettes. They were soldiers. My first instinct was to move away. Heidi pulled me toward them. I whispered, "What are you doing?"

She called, "Hello, boys!"

The soldiers whistled at her. She blushed and raised her skirt slightly. I just stared at the ground, trying to blend in with the snow. A soldier talked to her in German. She would laugh, smile, and wink at them, making them whistle and flirt more.

I was never good at flirting. Heidi seems to be a pro at it. She had the boys wrapped around her finger. It reminded me of Emma at school. She could flirt easily with any guy. All the boys liked her.

I decided I'd head back to the cottage. She noticed me leaving and pulled me back. She introduced me in German. The boys tipped their hats and spoke to me, but I had no clue what they were saying. Heidi nudged me and asked, "Well aren't you going to answer them?"

What was the question? I smiled awkwardly and said, "I'm not sure." The boys looked confused and so was Heidi. I stuttered. "Uh . . . I . . . I'm not feeling well. I'll go back to the house."

I broke away from her and ran back to the house. It felt good to have full control of my legs. I've never missed running this much. I didn't run far when Heidi started calling me back. I turned around to see if she was coming after me, and soon as I did that, I smacked into someone in front of me. I fell down onto the cold, snowy ground. I heard someone speak German. I felt a hand grab mine. I groaned and sat up, "Sorry, I didn't see you there."

I opened my eyes and gasped. It was the beautiful blonde soldier from the camp. He smiled at me. Does he know who I am? Was he going to arrest me? He helped me up. He said something in German again. I shook my head, "I can only speak Dutch."

He smiled, "Sorry that I knocked into you. It was my fault. I was distracted."

"Oh, it's ok. I'll be on my way!" I answered quickly, trying to move around him. "Sorry again!"

He blocked my path, his hypnotizing eyes digging into mine, "I was distracted by your beauty."

I felt my cheeks heat my face. I looked down sheepishly. If he only knew who I was, he wouldn't be saying that. I looked up at him. I'm surprised he doesn't remember me. I asked, "What's your name?"

He smiled, "John Krushak. I must know yours as well."

I answered, "Clara Steinenhauser."

He took my hand and kissed it. He looked me in the eyes. They were soft and kind. At the concentration camp, they were hard and piercing. He really didn't remember me. He asked softly, "Would you care to get a drink with me?"

I answered quickly, "Oh, I was about to head in for the night actually."

He nodded, "I see. Tomorrow then?"

He's persistent. I had no clue what to do, but Heidi sure did. She popped up next to me and replied cheerfully, "Of course she'd love to!"

He smiled wider, "Ok! Billy's Tavern at 9 p.m. Goodnight."

He shuffled through the snow to the other soldiers. Heidi giggled and hugged me. "Did you see how he was looking at you?"

I pushed her away, "Why did you do that?"

She replied, "So you could stay another night!"

"I don't know if I want to stay though," I said as we walked back to her cottage. "I'm still thinking about things."

She smirked, "Well you can stay another night and still think about it. Maybe your date tomorrow with that soldier will help you change your mind."

"Maybe and maybe not!" I exclaimed. "And it is not a date! We're just getting drinks."

Is it a date? I've never been on one, and I've never been asked on one. I've grown up more this past week than I have in my entire life!

We went back to Heidi's house. We sat on the couch, and she talked about the soldiers she had flirted with. She really reminded me of Emma now, talking about all the guys she really likes and the dates she's been on. It was hard to listen to her because she would be talking in Dutch, and then she would switch to German.

I wish my life could be normal like hers. If she only knew how my life was right now. What I've overcome and what I've seen. Then, she wouldn't care that shy Karl Schmidt won't talk to her, or ugly Ben Heiser keeps winking at her.

She yawned, "I'm getting tired, how about you?" We went to her bedroom, and she handed me a nightgown of hers. She's been so kind. I thanked her for all that she had done for me. She smiled and said goodnight. I told her I'd sleep on the couch tonight. She deserved to sleep in her own bed. This was her house after all. She gave me a pillow and some blankets, and I went to the living room.

I laid my head down on the soft pillow. I didn't feel tired at all. I thought about Devin and Kevin. I wonder if they were still alive. It'd be a miracle. However, my legs working are definitely a miracle. I can't stop wiggling my toes. I'm so happy.

I wonder what my "date" will be like tomorrow. It will be with John Krushak, the blonde soldier, of all people. I think he is very handsome, but what if he knows who I am. I could get in so much trouble for escaping. What if he only asked me on a date just to arrest me and send me back to the camp? If that happens it's the crematories for me. I felt my eyelids finally get heavy as I closed my eyes and went to sleep.

"Rise and shine!" laughed Heidi. I groaned and sat up stiffly. I watched Heidi skip and dance around the room. How could she have so much energy in the morning? "I know what you're thinking, but it isn't morning. You overslept. It's about noon right now. Ready for brunch?"

Noon? Brunch? My stomach growled. I said in a gravelly voice, "You bet I am."

She chuckled and skipped to the kitchen. I slowly stood up and stretched. Her couch wasn't as comfy as her bed. My back popped loudly. It reminded me of when I first got off the train. Anne had popped her back and smiled for the first time in days. I remembered how much joy that brought me to see her smile.

I shuffled into the kitchen. Heidi had prepared a lavish feast. Warm eggs and toast, crispy hash browns, schnitzel, red cabbage, and delicious sauerkraut! My mouth watered at the sight of it. I dashed to the table, ready to pile my plate with food.

Heidi chuckled at me eating, "I've never seen a girl eat as much as you do. You're very skinny. Did your father starve you?"

I stopped momentarily to think of a good lie, "Yes, actually. He was such a pig, stuffing himself all the time while I ate scraps."

She gave me a sympathetic look, "I'm sorry. It must've been hard, but you won't be abused like that anymore."

She hugged me. If she only knew who I was, she probably would be abusing me right now. I hugged her back. It is nice to have a friend on my side.

I helped clean her little cottage. It didn't take much time, although, it was hard work. We scrubbed the floors with a brush; hand washed all of the laundry and dusted her china. She talked about all the stuff she was going to do to me for my date. I kept reminding her that we were only going to get a couple of drinks, but she didn't listen.

"Oh, I should try some of my makeup on you. Our skin colors are similar. You should wear this lovely green dress I have. It would look so nice on you and along with these heels and—"

She blabbered on and on. I kept thinking about John. I hope he doesn't know who I am. Maybe he'll fall in love with me, and then I will have the new life I've wanted. Maybe if he loved me enough he would keep me safe, and it won't matter that I'm Jewish.

What am I thinking? That would be a horrible way to live with him! How did those thoughts get in my head? I shouldn't be thinking about those things. Maybe I should just ditch him and run as far as I can from this place.

We finished the chores and then ate dinner together. We had leftover brunch. She talked about the vacant cottages in the village. She suggested that after I get a job I should rent one. I didn't listen to her though. All I could hear was the sound of my terrified heart trembling inside my chest.

If he does find out who I am, I can't imagine how upset he will be. What if John gets so angry he tries to kill me? Oh, what will I do then? I felt the tears well up in my eyes. I couldn't let Heidi see me cry. She didn't seem to notice because she was talking so much.

I helped her clear the table and wash dishes. Now she was talking about what she'll do to my hair. Is she ever silent? She sent me to the bathroom to freshen up. As I scrubbed my hair, I thought about what I'd say on the date . . . I mean my get together with John. Should I think of a new identity to go with my new name?

I dried myself and looked in the mirror. I definitely don't look the same as I did at the hospital. I'm not as skinny, which for once I'm actually proud of. My skin and hair looked so much healthier. My hair had a gleaming shine to it and my skin glowed.

I put on a robe and walked to Heidi's room. Heidi set my clothes out on the bed. She saw me and smiled brightly, "Hello, gorgeous! I got your outfit laid out here."

She left to let me change. I put on the clothes. I actually looked good. I smiled and walked out to show Heidi. She gasped, "You look great! I haven't helped someone get ready for a date in a while. I forgot how much fun it is! I'll braid your hair and do your makeup, and then you'll be on your way."

As she braided my hair, she gave me date tips. I'm happy she did because I've never been on one. I remember Emma going on numerous dates. Mother always helped her get ready though. Anne and I just watched.

She started on my makeup, blabbering about her past dates. I tuned her out again. I decided to take it slow and easy. I don't want to get my hopes up. I actually hope it doesn't go well so I can get out of the village. She showed me a mirror, "You look fantastic!"

I gasped. My lips were dark red. My skin tone was absolutely flawless. My blonde eyelashes are black and much longer. My eyebrows were once fuzzy caterpillars, now they were even and trimmed nicely. My cheeks were a soft rose, and the scar on my forehead was barely visible

I smiled at her, "Thank you, Heidi, and if this works out maybe I'll stay. If it doesn't . . . well . . . I just want to be as far from my father as possible. It's a security thing, and I just don't want him to find me; if he's even looking for me . . . no hard feelings?"

She nodded, "I understand, Clara. You look great, and I'm sure he'll think you're spectacular. I'd love for you to stay though. We'd be great neighbors."

She gave me a coat and walked with me to the tavern. I felt very jittery, like I had little bubbles popping in my stomach. My heart fluttered. Why am I feeling like this? I never had fluttery feelings before. Am I sick?

She noticed my nervousness, "Let me walk you inside."

I opened the door for her and followed her inside the tavern. The tavern was lit only by candles that were on every table. A man waved at Heidi and said something in German. She laughed and replied back. She seemed to know most of the men here. She smiled and joked around with each man.

We sat down at the bar. A man approached us and spoke in German. Heidi smiled at me, "What are you getting?"

I have never had an alcoholic beverage. I didn't know what kind to order either. I remember at my cousin Tiffany's wedding they had champagne. I said, "A glass of champagne please."

The man cocked his head. Heidi laughed, "Oh, Clara, they don't have that here! I'll order you something."

She talked to the man. He nodded and started filling glasses with alcohol. She smiled at me, "That's Billy, the owner of the tavern."

I looked around for John. Maybe he won't show up, and then I can leave in anger that he didn't show! Suddenly, the door opened, and a tall man walked inside the tavern. It was John. His blonde hair sparkled with fresh snow, and his eyes searched around the tavern. Heidi nudged me, "I'll move a few seats down. If you get uncomfortable or something, just let me know, and I'll get you out alright?"

I hugged her quickly, "Thank you so much, Heidi."

She smiled, "You're welcome, Clara. Oh, here he comes! Good luck!"

She jumped up and walked down the bar area. I turned to see John towering above me. He smiled, took my hand and kissed it. I blushed as he sat down. He ordered a drink. Billy handed me my drink. I took a sip and choked.

John patted my back. He asked in a concerned voice in German. I guess he's asking if I'm ok. I nodded, "Oh . . . *cough* . . . I'm fine. I've never had this drink before. Oh, and remember I only speak Dutch."

John smiled, "I forgot about that, sorry. I usually just get a beer. So how did you learn Dutch so well?"

"I had a very good teacher in my school. I do know German. I am German . . . no doubt about that."

He looked at me funny and chuckled, "Of course you are!"

That lie was the beginning of my new false identity. I became Clara Steinenhauser. I lived in this village all my life, and I have two brothers and three sisters; Daniel, Karl, Mary, Margret, and Marianne. I hate tomatoes and have a fear of goats.

John talked about his life. He has two sisters and four brothers; Laura, Maura, Jason, Jackson, Jeffery, and Joseph. His mother died giving birth to his youngest brother, Joseph, and his father tried his best to support them. He loved his father dearly for being strong for them.

If he only knew about my Papa, how I felt the same way for him, maybe that'll stop him the next time he takes another life. I felt my eyes water, and I wiped them casually.

"So where do you work?" he asked.

"Here in fact," I said quickly. I looked over at Billy. He was assisting another customer. I looked back at John. "I've worked here for many years. It's a great job."

He gave me a half smile, "Funny, I've been here many times, but I've never seen you here. I haven't even seen you anywhere in the village."

I think that was the wrong lie. I had to get us off topic. I smiled sweetly, "I live outside of the village. I like the view of the countryside. It's very quiet and peaceful."

He nodded slowly, but he still had a small glint of doubt in his eyes. Does he know? Is it my scar? Has it become visible? I covered up my forehead with my hand, pretending to massage my temples. He said, "I work at a concentration camp not too far from here. Have you heard of it? I learned Dutch from a few soldiers and doctors there."

The words "concentration camp" made me flinch. Those words will always make me flinch. I tried to act casual, "Not really."

He began talking about the camp, going into things I've never heard of. He explained that the camp was more of a test camp. They perform many tests on the Jews. He talked about some of the tests they performed such as removing limbs from Jews' bodies. They sometimes put them in pressure chambers to simulate what it is like being in an airplane. The test usually resulted in the subject's eyes popping out of their skull. They'd throw them into pools of freezing water to see how long it takes for them to die.

Every sentence he said was like a punch to my stomach. I couldn't imagine all of the Jews being tortured in so many inhumane ways. John's eyes lit up as he told stories of how he and his fellow soldiers would execute the Jews. The blue fire of his eyes burned me. I wanted to kill him just as he killed many other Jews. Why did I think it would be ok if he fell in love with me? He was disgusting, so sadistic and cruel.

I want to run far from this village, no . . . more than that. I want to run from this country! From this world! I want to escape from all the fighting and war and anger that everyone has generated. I just want peace!

"Clara? You're clenching your fists. Are you ok?" John asked.

I glared at him. Remembering who I'm supposed to be, I unclenched my fists and smiled, "I was just thinking . . . uh." His eyes seemed to sparkle as I looked into his eyes. I heard a thought pop into my head. "Would you like to dance?"

"Sure!" he exclaimed.

Did I say that out loud? What was I thinking? Great! Why would I ask that? I want to kill this guy now I'm going to dance with him.

He walked me to the dance floor, and we danced slowly. His eyes met mine again. Another thought came into my head. "Flap your arms like a chicken."

Well that's a silly thought! Why am I thinking that?

"What are you doing?" laughed Heidi from the bar. I realized my arms were flapping up and down as if I were trying to fly. I wish I could; everyone started to laugh at me. I gasped, astonished that I did what my thoughts told me to do. I looked at John. He had a smirk on his face.

I stopped flapping and resumed dancing with him. I asked, "Why weren't you laughing? Didn't you think I was funny?"

He replied coolly, "I can't believe you did that."

I looked him in the eye. They seemed to speak to me like a conscience. They were telling me how to dance. I felt like I was soaring around the room with John. I said astounded, "I can't believe I'm doing this. I don't know how to dance very well."

"Obviously you're lying because you are doing very well," he replied in a smooth and even tone. "You're the one who asked me to dance in the first place."

This was true. I tried to put together the pieces of the puzzle. John gave me a mysterious smile as I stared at his face, trying to solve it. He grinned, "Give up?"

"Are you responsible for me doing that stuff?" I asked.

He nodded, "My grandfather was a magician and a hypnotist. He showed me a few tricks."

I was completely baffled. I chuckled, "Just when I thought I figured you out."

He laughed, "Sometimes I use it on the Jews. This one girl, she almost looks like you. Her hair was blonde, and her eyes were very blue. She was sent to the hospital for experiments. She wouldn't stop screaming and trying to get away. I made her calm down with hypnotism."

I realized that the girl he was talking about was me. I tried to smile and pretend that I was intrigued. He continued, "I also use it to torture them. I was supervising a group of Jewish workers building a barrack. I made one think that bees were swarming him. He fell from the top of the building trying to get away. It was hilarious watching him flap about!"

He let out a hearty laugh. I had to force myself to laugh along. We continued to dance. I tried not to think about the Jewish worker, but I couldn't help it. How could a person laugh about killing another man with his mind?

Soon my feet started to hurt, and we sat down. We drank more, and my thoughts became fuzzy. I made up stories about my fake family. He laughed at all of my fake stories. I almost forgot how sick of a person he was.

It became late, and I told John I needed to go home. I winked at Heidi as I walked by her. She smiled and waved. When we walked outside, John turned me to face him. I felt slightly dizzy. He held me close and looked down at me. His crystal eyes gleamed at me. I heard a thought in my mind say, "Kiss me."

Should I resist him? I looked at his lips. They looked so inviting and perfect. I couldn't control myself. I gave in and kissed him. His lips were warm and soft. He pulled me closer and deepened the kiss.

In that moment, my life was complete. I finally thought I had it figured out. I'd have a little house close to Heidi's. It would be the perfect little cottage. Maybe I could get used to John. We could be soul mates if I give it time. Perhaps I'll marry John and start my new life here. Maybe I'll have a few kids too. What would I name them? I've always liked the name Belle for a girl. If I had a boy I'd name him after James.

I pulled my lips away, "John, I have something to tell you. My name isn't Clara it is Jenna." I said slowly. I didn't want to live the rest of my life being known as "Clara."

He murmured, "Jenna is a pretty name. Why would you lie to me about that?"

"Well—"

"Hmm . . . Jenna. Where have I heard that before? It reminds me of a file I was looking at. It was about the same girl I hypnotized at the hospital."

I gulped. I am that girl. I'm Jenna, and I'm Jewish.

His eyes narrowed, then he gasped, "Wait a minute."

"What?" I asked as innocently as possible

He said in shock, "You're the girl . . . you're the Jewish girl."

My children were disappearing; Belle and James. I hastily denied it, "No what are you talking about?"

He pulled me closer. Our faces were inches from each other. His eyes pierced my mind. He kept asking me over and over. Who are you? Who are you? I couldn't take it anymore, "My name is Jenna Altsman, and I'm a Jew!"

He yelled something in German and threw me to the ground. He hissed, "You stay there."

He ran into the tavern. I'm definitely not staying here! I quickly kicked off my heels; I can run faster without them on my feet. I got up and ran from the tavern. I flew by the little cottages I will never live in. I heard people chasing me. They were shouting after me. I heard John's voice over all of them.

"Jew!" he cried. "Catch it!"

It. He called me *it.* I felt the tears streaming down my face. Minutes ago he was kissing me and thinking he loved me. Now he wants me dead.

I felt myself slowing down. I was so tired. I kept trying to move faster, willing my legs to move quicker. They were sluggish from the alcohol. I'll never drink again if I can get away!

I felt strong arms grab me by the waist. I screamed as the person threw me to the ground. I looked up to see John. He yelled and kicked me in the stomach. I groaned and cried, begging him to stop. He kicked me in the legs, stomach, and face.

More people joined him. A man punched me square in the jaw. I felt it pop, and I let out a howl. No one cared; all they cared about was kicking me and making sure my body was completely worthless. Even little children joined in by grabbing my hair and yanking it hard. I shrieked and tried to slap them away, but it was no use.

Two men grabbed my arms and held me against a tree. My eyes were drooping and swelling. Women slapped me with cold rags. The stinging cold rags made my face burn. The cool air chilled my face and made it burn worse. I begged for them to stop. A woman grabbed the hem of my dress and ripped it. Others joined until my green dress was ripped into a green rag.

John approached me grimly. He spat in my face and growled, "You are a liar, a filthy Jewish liar. Your whole disgusting race is. You deserve to die right now, but I'll take you back to the concentration camp so you can die with your race."

A truck pulled up to us. The siren turned off and two burly men stepped out of the truck. The two men holding me handed me off to them. Before they threw me into the back of the truck, John took my face into his hands. His eyes searched my face. Will he change his mind and set me free? I heard a thought in my head, "I hope you rot with the maggots."

I'm tired of all these threats. I spat into his eye, see how he liked that. He scowled and squeezed my face hard. I did my best not show the pain on my face, but it was difficult. He released his grip and barked orders at the men. The two men dragged me to the truck. I glared at John the whole time. They threw me into the chamber in the back. The only opening was the barred door, but I could barely stick my hand through it. I pressed my face up against the bars. I yelled as loud as I could, "John, you kissed a Jew and you liked it! You loved me! How does that feel?"

John stared back at me solemnly. The rest of the villagers screamed threats at me. It looked like chaos. I didn't see Heidi there. Good. I didn't want this to be the last thing she would remember me by. Heidi was so nice to me. Maybe I should've told her the truth. I shook my head and shuffled into the corner of the truck.

Trash and glass bottles were thrown at me. I tried to dodge it, but fragments of glass scattered across the floor. I stayed huddled in my little corner. I wish I could melt into the corner and never be seen again.

The truck jolted, and I bounced into the air. I tried to lie down and sleep, but the road was bumpy. The cold snow blew through the barred door, sweeping under my torn dress and making me shiver. I sat up and ran my hands through my hair.

Why can't they leave me alone? What did I ever do to deserve this treatment? I didn't do too many horrible things. I cheated on my math exam once and sometimes I said rude things to Mother behind her back, but I never did anything so awful to deserve this! I'm not sure what started all the mistreatment of my race, but I'm sure we don't deserve it!

I felt the truck jolt to a stop. I heard soldiers yelling and arguing. Footsteps stomped to the back of the truck. A soldier growled at me, "Looks like you'll be spending the night in the truck, Jew."

I snapped, "I have a name. It's Jenna!"

He pointed his gun at me and snarled, "I should shoot you now, but I have strict orders to take you back to the concentration camp. Alive."

"You should just kill me, might as well get it over with," I mumbled, moving towards the door.

He laughed, "Stupid girl. I hope you enjoy staying the night in the truck. Did you know it is supposed to get 10 below tonight? Perhaps you'll get your wish and freeze to death."

He walked away laughing. I grabbed the bars and shook them; wishing they would break, and then I'd make my great escape. The cold wind blew fragments of ice into my face. I shuddered and moved further back. Will I make it through the night?

Chapter Seventeen

I examined my toes. They were blue and stiff. I was scared to touch them. What if they just snap off? They felt like they would if I just wiggled a toe. Snowflakes covered my hair. I was so frozen it hurt to even move my eyes. It felt like they were freezing into little eyeball ice cubes!

Falling asleep was impossible. I had stayed up most of the night, battling the cold blizzard. Snow had piled up in my little chamber, taking up the whole space. I was forced into a little corner.

I remembered being locked up in the truck with my family. We were cramped up in a tiny chamber like this. I remember the despair of everyone in the truck like the crying baby and the angry, old man. I remember Papa telling us to be brave. He told me to take care of Anne. He wouldn't be proud of me now.

I felt tears stream down my cold cheeks. The wind blew onto them and froze my tears. I rubbed my cheeks. My hands were so cold they burned my face. I felt the icy tears fall off my skin.

I tilted my head slightly and heard a snapping sound. I looked down on the floor. A small lock of my hair had snapped off my head. It lied stiffly on the floor. I hugged myself closer and shivered. My hair is snapping off, my tears are freezing on my cheeks, and my cold hands burn my face. Some winter wonderland this place is. I shut my eyes tightly, hoping I could possibly sleep.

I heard the sound of birds chirping. The constant blow of cold wind had finally settled down. Thank goodness the blizzard was finally over!

But something was wrong. I couldn't see anything. My eyes were literally frozen shut! I could barely crack open an eye. I sat up stiffly. My eyes were sealed shut from tears. I tried blinking. I rubbed my eyes, trying to break the ice. When I blinked, I could only open my right eye. When I did, I automatically shut it. The snow blinded me. I only had my right eye open for a millisecond, and all I could see was white. It covered the entire floor.

I hesitantly opened both my eyes. I squinted at the white blanket of snow that enveloped me. Snow covered me to my chest. I pushed the piles away from my body. My body was blue, and my fingernails were purple.

My tattered rags weren't keeping me dry. The snow had seeped through, and I was totally soaked. I shivered and wished for nice pair of corduroy pants and a warm sweater. I wouldn't even mind wearing that itchy hospital robe again. At least I'd have something dry covering my body.

I heard a commotion outside. A soldier appeared in front of the door. He growled at me, "You're coming out."

He opened the door. I couldn't believe it. Was he letting me go? I slowly moved out. He didn't help me down. I jumped out and landed on my knees. I stood up awkwardly. The harsh wind swept under my torn dress and made it rise. I pushed the rags down to cover myself up. The soldier didn't seem to care. He pushed me forward, "Move it!"

Where am I supposed to go? I looked at him, perplexed. He sighed, as if he were explaining instructions to a two year old, "The truck is stuck. The camp is 8 miles away. We're walking with the others to the camp. Now move!"

What others? He pushed me again. This time, I fell to the ground. I felt an arm grab me. I looked up to see a tired girl looking back at me. She was very tall and lanky. Her head was bald, and she wore baggy striped clothes. The girl pulled me up and led me to a herd of marching women.

I looked at my new surroundings. We were still in a snowy forest. Soldiers walked in ditches in case a woman tried to run. They were armed with guns. I gulped hard. Hopefully they won't use one on me.

The women marched along trying to keep up a good pace. However, if the soldiers didn't think they were quick enough, they'd kick them or knock them down. Then, they'd bark at them to get up and pick up the pace. I could tell none of the women were marching fast enough for the soldiers. Most of them had bruises on the backs of their legs from the soldiers' kicks.

The women wore the same uniform of striped clothes. None of them had shoes or hair. They didn't even have hats to cover their cold, bald heads.

The cold snow crunched between my toes. I wanted to cry out in pain. I looked down at the girl's feet. She was missing her pinky toes on both of her feet. She noticed me gaping at her feet. She said softly, "Frostbite. I had to remove them. My name is Camelia."

"Jenna," I whispered back.

"Why were you in that truck?" she asked.

"No talking!" snapped a soldier. He kicked Camelia in the back of the legs. She tumbled to the ground. I helped her up quickly. She smiled at me and mouthed, "Thanks."

We marched on through the snow. My feet became numb. It reminded me of back when I was in the hospital with my numb legs. I hated the numb feeling because it reminded me of all the memories there, mainly James.

A woman in front of me stumbled to the ground wheezing. Camelia jumped into action and tried to help her up. The woman pushed her away, hacking up blood. Some of the blood splattered onto Camelia's uniform. A soldier barked at Camelia to move. I grabbed her arm and led her away.

She had tears in her eyes. She looked behind at the woman. I did too. The woman gazed at her and then laid her head on the ground. She didn't move again. Camelia sobbed and clutched my hand. I asked, "Who is that?"

She whimpered, "My mother. She is . . . well . . . *was* the only family I had left. My father and my brother were separated from us. My sister, Julie, didn't make it through the first few days in the concentration camp. She was only 12 years old."

I held her hand tightly. I understood how she felt. She sobbed, "My mother and I had gotten into a fight before we left the camp. She wouldn't talk to me at all. I wish I could've told her I loved her . . . and that I'm sorry." She sniffled. "It's sad when you lose someone that you're so close to. Someone you love so much, but you never really showed it or told them daily. I talked to Julie about everything. I have told her I loved her before, yet I still didn't even come close to truly expressing how I really loved her. You don't know how important it is to tell them until they're gone."

She walked as close as she could to me to keep warm, but I could barely feel her body heat. She put her arm around me and sniffled into my ear. I whispered, "Why are all these women walking?"

She murmured, "We're on a death march. We're moving to different camps." Her grip around my waist tightened. It reminded me of when Anne and I would walk in the park. She would wrap her arms around me, and we would talk about everything and anything. I almost felt comforted.

I asked, "Is this your second camp?"

"Yes, and my last. I'm sure of it. I'm happy to die. No one will make fun of me for who I am anymore. It will be nice not to be bullied and tortured."

"I guess so. I don't like being bullied for being Jewish either."

"Jewish?" she asked.

"Yes. Aren't you?"

She looked me in the eye. Her eyes were bleary and red. They had a look of shock, but then they softened. She smiled sweetly and whispered in my ear, "No, I am a lesbian."

Chapter Eighteen

I broke away from her embrace, "Excuse me?"

She frowned, "You came from the same camp as me didn't you?"

I shook my head, "No I—"

I felt a blow to my back. I tumbled to the ground. I heard a soldier yell in my ear, "No talking!"

Camelia pulled me up and dragged me along with her. It began to snow again. I felt the flakes settle into my hair. I kept wiping my head and licking my wet hands for extra water. I even sucked the water from my wet hair. I didn't get much water, but it was better than nothing.

Camelia whispered in my ear, "We'll rest in another half mile or so. Keep up, Jenna!"

I stumbled along beside her. She tried to hold my hand to help me keep up with her, but it was too awkward to me. I let go of her hand each time she tried. It felt too weird. I've never been around a lesbian before.

I looked at the other women. I couldn't believe they were all lesbians, or were they? Was it just Camelia and a few others, or was this a total lesbian camp? I wish I could ask her, but my back was killing me, and I don't want to end up dead in the snow.

The soldiers made us halt. They let us sit in the snow and rest. Although my feet were killing me, I didn't sit down. My clothes were still damp, and I didn't want them to get worse. That didn't stop the other women. They plopped to the ground like sacks of potatoes.

Camelia stood next to me. She smiled at me, "So what's your story? You're not a lesbian?"

"No I'm not. I used to be in a hospital with a bunch of other kids. They had performed experiments on me and other children. I had escaped with a good friend, James, but he didn't make it. I almost died in the woods, but a man had rescued me. I stayed with him until I got better, and then I left him because he was a little crazy. I traveled to a small village and stayed with a nice lady, but I was caught by a soldier. They were driving me back to the camp, but the truck got stuck in a snow drift."

She nodded, "I see. I'm sorry if I made you feel uncomfortable. I thought you were part of my camp."

"Are all the women here lesbians?" I asked

"Yes. Well, most of them I suppose. My sister wasn't and neither was my mother. Some women who weren't lesbian were forced to go on the march because the soldiers thought they were lying and sent them with us."

"Why did your mother come with you on the march?"

"The news of the death march had come, and they said a majority of the lesbians and a few of the younger children will go. I had told my mother that I have to go on the march. She got very mad at me because our family is very strict Catholics. She had wanted me to lie and pretend to be someone I'm not. I'd rather die as myself then to maybe live on as someone I'm not. She didn't want me to go alone, so she had come with me. I wish she hadn't though."

She looked down and brushed a tear away from her face. I nodded and looked down too. She said softly, "I'm happy Julie didn't see her die. She was always very sensitive. She was in so much pain at the camp. The soldiers had thought she was a lesbian and taunted her often. She was so confused and scared. At night, I had heard all the women in my barracks cry, but her cries are what hurt me the most. She didn't last very long there. A soldier had hit her with the butt of his gun, and she tumbled down into a ditch. They didn't even bother recovering her body."

She kept sobbing softly. Her tears were freezing against her cheeks. I didn't want to watch her cry about her deceased family like this. I wiped the frozen tears off her face and brushed the snow off her shoulders and head. I suggested, "Maybe we should change the subject."

She nodded, "Tell me about your family." Not the direction I wanted this to go. I tugged on my rags. She smiled sadly. "Oh, you must be colder than me. I'm sorry, but I don't have any extra clothes. I don't think the soldiers will give you any either."

I forced a smile and said sarcastically, "Oh well it's only snowing."

She laughed softly, "Yeah, only snowing."

When I looked down at my feet, they had a blue tint to them. I'm too scared to touch them. Would they fall off like Camelia's toes? Do they just snap off like a falling leaf? I decided to avoid my curiosity about my feet.

The soldiers commanded us to move. I felt like my feet were solid blocks of cement. It hurt to lift them. The icy snow bit my feet and made them burn with coldness. Is it possible for your feet to be so cold that they're burning? If so that's what my feet felt like.

Camelia was worse than me. She doesn't have her pinky toes, and it makes her a little off balance. She bumped into me a lot. I let her grip my arm as a support.

The road seemed to go on for miles. Almost every 100 feet or so, a woman fell down and didn't get up. Camelia tried to help every one of them back up. I tried to help too, but every woman we tried to help didn't want to get up again.

It hurts me every time I try to help a woman. One woman fell down, and I ran to her side. I whispered, "You can make it! I'll help you up."

Her breaths came out in short gasps. She gasped, "I can't. I just can't anymore. Go away."

"Yes, you can!" I encouraged. "I believe in you. There's still hope."

"Sweet girl, there was never hope," she let out her last breath.

I heard fast footsteps approach me. I looked up to see an angry soldier. He kicked me over and barked, "Move before I beat you into the ground!"

I quickly stood up and caught up to Camelia. I told her about the woman, and she nodded sadly, "None of them believe there's hope. Do you believe, Jenna?"

I didn't know how to answer. I saw another woman fall. Even though I knew she would deny help, I ran to her side, "Get up! You can make it."

She whispered, "Oh, I will make it. I'm going to trick these stupid soldiers. They'll just walk right by me; I'm certain of it. Just you wait, dearie. If you were smart, you'd follow my example. Now shoo!"

I caught up to Camelia. She sighed, "I guess she didn't make it."

I glanced back at the drift. A group of soldiers peered at her body, shrugged their shoulders, and walked away. She did it! She tricked them! I nudged Camelia, and she turned around and saw the snow drift. She looked at me with a puzzled look on her face. I whispered, "She's alive."

Her eyes widened, and she looked back at the drift. I glanced at the drift too. A stray soldier peered at the woman in the snow drift. He grimaced and positioned his gun at her. I heard a high pitched squeal of protest. I had turned back around before I heard the shots fire. I'm glad I didn't see the blood spew from the drift like an erupting volcano.

That's how Camelia described it. She gazed at the drift too long. I felt her head press against my shoulder. She sobbed silently. I noticed soldiers watching us. I gently pushed Camelia away. She looked at me teary eyed. I nodded behind us at the soldiers. She nodded and broke away from me.

Camelia walked until she was a couple of feet ahead of me. I soon found myself walking alongside a young girl. She had big, brown eyes. She was very short, and her head bobbled slightly while she walked. She looked very familiar, like one of Anne's friends. She noticed me and lit up, "Jenna?

Is that you? It's me, Paula, Anne's friend."

I knew it! I whispered, "Hi, Paula. It's a relief to find someone I know."

She smiled and nodded. I slowly remembered Paula. She came to our old house often to stay the night with Anne. She was a sweet girl. They were very similar. Her hair was even as shiny and dark as Anne's.

I gazed at her shiny, bald head. It broke my heart to see all of her beautiful hair gone. She shivered and walked closer to me. I wondered if she was a lesbian too. If she was, I wonder if Anne knew. She would've told me if one of her friends was a lesbian. I asked quietly, "Paula, this may be an uncomfortable question for you, but are you a lesbian?"

It felt awkward for me to ask a young girl that. It's awkward to ask anyone that! She shook her head, "No, why do you ask?"

I sighed a little, "I just made friends with a girl that's in this camp. She had said most of the women in the camp are lesbian and that's why you're on the death march. Do you know Camelia?"

She nodded, "Yes. I knew she's a lesbian, but I'm not; I'm Polish."

"What? I didn't know Polish people were here too."

She nodded, "Yeah, lots of us are here. I'm here because I'm too young to do the work in the camp. I'll probably be gassed when I get to the camp, if I even make it."

I gasped, "Don't speak like that!"

"It's the truth," she growled. I widened my eyes. Paula's personality swerved. "I had watched my younger sisters, Ruta and Sara, walk into a gas chamber. It didn't take too long. I had watched them while I stood naked in a line with other women. I was moved into a barrack with 200 other women. I had shared my small bed with five girls. Two of them had wet the bed the first night. One of them had even started her period right next to me. I had smelled like pee and blood in the morning, and we didn't have showers. I dug holes every day. They were filled with dying bodies. Some of them were still alive when they were thrown inside the pit. They had suffocated between the bodies. I had watched that happen, Jenna. My hair was infested with lice my first week there. They had shaved me after that. My clothes were too big on me, and my pants always fell down. The soldiers would pull them down just to humiliate me. I've experienced things a 10 year old should never experience. In fact, I feel like I've aged another 10 years on this march."

I was in shock. Her story was horrible. I said, "I'm so sorry, Paula, I didn't know. I can't believe what we've all been through. I was tested on at a crazy hospital with other children. I watched some of my friends there die or get mutated! I almost lost my legs too."

She raised her eyebrows, "That's awful. I'm sorry too, Jenna. I shouldn't have made my life sound worse than yours. I bet you've seen some bad things too."

I chuckled, "Oh if you only knew."

I remembered all of my friends. Poor Devin and Kevin will forever be intertwined. Kristen drowned in her worst fears, and Kelly became insane. Jacob's eyes were removed, and James died saving me.

I looked at Paula. She had an easy look on her face and a sparkle in her eyes. She doesn't have a clue what I've seen. I should have bragging rights. She wouldn't believe the emotions I've felt the past week.

Should I tell her? Why shouldn't I? She thinks she's seen life? Has she seen someone kill her best friend? See if she crawls into a little hole and cries like I've wanted to all this time? Watch the little sparkle in her eyes dull like mine has?

I shook my head. What was I thinking? I'm not like this. I looked at Paula again. She still had a peaceful look on her face. She was brave as she calmly walked to her death. I followed her like a faithful sheep, following my shepherd to certain death.

Chapter Nineteen

I want to chop my legs off. That thought occurred to me as we approached the camp. I couldn't believe I would think that, especially since I've almost lost my legs. I've walked 8 miles in a day. I'm malnourished, breathless and weak. My muscles burned intensely. My body wants to collapse to the ground.

The soldiers lined us up. They got us in order so they could escort us into the camp. It felt like the day we had gotten off the train, except this time we're wearing clothes. Not the best clothes in my case.

Paula panted next to me. Her scrawny chest heaved up and down. The air was freezing cold. She coughed hard and spat up phlegm and blood. The blood contrasted with the white snow.

She was bent over her mess. I patted her back, hoping the soldiers wouldn't notice her. Too late. A soldier kicked her backside, and she fell into her mess. She lied still in the bloody snow. The soldier laughed at her and walked away. Another soldier barked at me to pick her up. I quickly pulled her to her feet. The phlegm stuck to her shirt, and the blood stained her face and neck. The soldier spat at us and continued down the line.

Camelia appeared next to me. She helped me hold Paula steady. Our hands touched briefly. She blushed and smiled at me. I looked back at her and gave her a half smile. She whispered in my ear, "Jenna, of all the women here that will die with us, I'm happy I'm dying with you."

She kissed my cheek. I took a step back. That was the first time a girl has ever kissed me. I felt my cheeks heat up. She said quickly, "I know you aren't a lesbian, but I want to tell you you're beautiful. I'm sure I'm scaring you and making you feel awkward, but that's how I feel."

I wish people would stop telling me things before they die. I nodded, "I'm glad you got that off your chest. Yes, you do scare me, but I'm glad you spoke your mind. You're very brave, Camelia."

She blushed and smiled shyly. Paula wobbled slightly. She murmured, "I'm not going to make it to the gas chambers. I feel so horrible. Thank you for helping me though."

Camelia rubbed Paula's bald head. She smiled slightly, "Hey, that's what friends are for. We're sticking together. We won't die alone."

"You're right. Hey, Jenna, where are Emma and Anne? Or are they?" Paula stopped talking.

I replied coldly, "Anne is dead. Emma might be too."

Paula trembled and hugged me. Camelia gave me a sympathetic smile and hugged me too. The soldiers came back, and I pushed them away quickly. They understood and turned away. They walked by us without a second glance.

I sighed in relief. I grabbed my blonde hair and twisted and twirled it. Will this be the last time I ever play with my hair? Was this the last moment of my life?

I'm not sure. I'm happy to be dying with two, nice girls, but I'd rather it be James or Anne. James was my closest friend through all of this, and Anne was my little sister. Sadly, they died before me, and I still didn't tell them everything I needed to say. I fully understood why Camelia and Paula were acting like this. They wanted all their burdens and thoughts off their chest before they died.

The soldiers finally led us inside the camp. We marched past the barracks. I looked longingly for Emma and Mother. I wonder if they were still alive. I wonder if they're still here. They could've been forced on a death march.

I felt a hand grasp mine tightly. It was Paula. She looked me in the eye. She was tearing up, "I'm scared."

I squeezed her hand. Camelia grabbed my other hand, "I see the gas chambers ahead. This is it."

My life will be over soon. The end of Jenna Isabella Altsman was finally here. I held my friends' hands as the soldiers led us to the gas chamber. They instructed us to take off our clothes. I felt the déjà vu creep in. Memories of stripping clothes off with Emma and Mother had come into my mind. I remember I had to help Anne because she was so scared and confused. That was so long ago.

Paula began to cry. I helped her take off her huge shirt. She wailed and screamed. The realization that she will die was finally sinking in. I sat on my knees and held her face. She sniffled and hiccupped. I saw Anne's face in place of hers. I almost fell backwards in shock. I looked her in the eye and said sternly, "My papa once told me that you need to be strong and brave when you are weak and scared. I want you to do that for me."

She nodded and choked on her tears. I stood back up and finished taking my clothes off. When I was finished, Camelia averted her eyes. She avoided looking at me. I took her hand and said softly, "You don't have to do that. It doesn't matter anymore."

She turned to look at me. She kept her eyes on my face. Her eyes told me everything. Her face reminded me of Emma's; completely relaxed and cool. She was ready.

I checked on Paula. She had a calmer look on her face too. It reminded me of Anne's face before the hammer came swinging down on her. She was ready.

I blinked a tear out. I never thought I would die like this. I had always imagined I'd peacefully die in bed with a smile on my face. Instead, I'll die in a room packed full of people and deadly gas fumes. I'll die hearing the screams of dying people ringing in my ears.

I also can't get over James and I having a new life. That idea still stays in my mind along with the ideas of staying in the village with Heidi and John. All my ideas and dreams were crushed by Nazis. One group of people had the power to destroy all of my dreams.

I watched the other women. They were hugging each other and bawling. Some of the soldiers harassed them; touching them and insulting them. I'm tired of seeing that. This time I'm ready to die. I'm ready to end it all. No more running away. No more stressing if Mother and Emma are ok. No more wishing my friends were still alive because I'll be with them shortly. I'm ready.

The soldiers sent us inside the chamber. We were in the middle of the line. We were almost there. I gripped my friends' hands. They squeezed my hands back. For once, I felt completely happy. A smile appeared on my face.

Suddenly, I felt a strong hand grip my shoulder. I turned around and screamed in horror. Dr. Vinkleman glared down at me, "Hello, Jenna, glad you could come back. Ready for your surgery?"

Before I could say a word, he pulled me out of line. Camelia and Paula screamed and grabbed my hands. The soldiers hit them with the butt of their guns. They screamed my name. I heard it over the pounding of my heart. I screamed, "No! Camelia and Paula! Be strong and brave for me!"

They shook their heads and protested. They pushed the soldiers, but they didn't move an inch. I kept repeating what I said. Finally, Camelia understood and held Paula back. Paula tried to fight Camelia, but she soon gave up. They bawled and held onto each other as the soldiers pushed them inside the chamber. They would die without me.

My voice was cracking, but that didn't stop me from screaming. I heard Dr. Vinkleman mumble something about removing my vocal chords. I didn't care. I was freeing my emotions. I wanted everyone in this camp to know how furious I was. Dr. Vinkleman became angry with me. He stopped walking and held me still. He positioned me so I was facing the gas chamber, "You can watch your pathetic friends die, Jew."

I watched the soldiers slam the door shut. Two men inserted something from the top of the building. It must be the chemical that will kill everyone inside the gas chamber. There had to have been at least 400 women and children inside the gas chamber.

Suddenly, I heard the screams. I couldn't make out what they were saying. After a few minutes, the screams slowly faded away. I fell to my knees. My red, crusty eyes couldn't shed anymore tears. I just moaned and shook my head. This was wrong. This mass slaughter was completely inhumane, and I had just witnessed it.

I felt a sharp yank on my hair. Dr. Vinkleman yanked my hair again. He laughed, "First, I'll shave your pretty hair off."

Soldiers guarded us. He led me through the dirty barracks area where curious Jews peered out from the doors. The soldiers barked at them and they disappeared. I was still bawling. My tired legs couldn't walk anymore.

I fell to the ground, and he still continued to pull me by my long hair. I can't do this anymore! I clawed at the ground and screamed for God to kill me now. I tried to pull my hair away from him, but he kicked me in the face and continued pulling me.

My eye swelled up. I knew it would be a black eye soon. I couldn't see very well. The tears blinded my eyes. I wanted to shut them so badly.

I'm glad I didn't.

A woman walked out of a barrack. She started pushing a wheelbarrow full of dead bodies. Her bony fingers clenched the handles as she used all of her energy to push. Her tattered uniform hung on her scrawny shoulders. Her dirty, bald head had a few scratches on it.

I knew who it was.

Emma.

She solemnly looked at me. I saw her lips part in surprise. I felt my heart beat faster. I missed her face so much. Her eyes began to glow like they used to when she saw me, but they were quickly dimmed by the presence of a soldier. He barked orders at her. He beckoned her towards him. She set the wheelbarrow down, and walked to him.

I wanted to call out to her. I wanted to tell her I loved her and ask if she knew where Mother was and if she's ok. I wanted to tell her all the things I've experienced and how I almost escaped and died.

I opened my mouth, but nothing came out. She moved out of my sight.

Would that be the last time I see her? Will I ever see Mother again? I had to keep my eyes open. I fought the pain and squinted around. Do I want to see Mother? Would she want to see me? She would break down and the soldiers would beat her, but I need to see her.

My heart stopped when I looked down at the bodies in the wheelbarrow. I saw Mother crumpled under other bodies. Her face was scratched up and flies were all over her. A fly landed on her unblinking eye. I felt the urge to throw up, but I held it in.

She's gone. My mother is dead. I slowly closed my eyes and let the feeling pass through. The tears squeezed out of my eyes. I never thought I'd lose her like this. No one ever thinks their mother will die from something like this. I thought about all the other kids who watched their mothers get beaten and violated. All the kids who watched their mothers starve to death to keep them alive for another day. I opened my eyes and saw other women being loaded into the wheelbarrow and carted away.

That's the last time I saw Mother.

Dr. Vinkleman and I arrived at the hospital. As soon as I saw the building, I started to fight him again. I felt like I had rested long enough, but I was still weak and sore. He jerked my head every time I resisted him. He dragged me inside the hospital and shouted orders to the nurses. He let go of my hair and continued to give orders.

I was sprawled out on the floor. I sat up quickly and tried to run for it. A nurse with a white mask took my hand and pulled me to a room. I pushed her away and tried to run, but she easily caught my arm again and kept pulling me to the room. I couldn't see her face because of the mask. She made me sit in a cold chair. I knew what was going to happen.

No way in hell was she getting my hair.

Something inside me changed. I'm not a violent person. I've never wanted to hurt anyone. I've stayed out of trouble. I'm the good girl, but now that's over. I'll stop at nothing to keep my hair on my head. If they do take it, I will stop at nothing to give them hell. I will not stop kicking and screaming. I will never stop fighting. My whole attitude changed that moment.

She pulled out the shears, but I was already out of the chair and halfway to the door. I tripped into the hallway. I looked side to side. Nurses ran towards me. I've got to get out of here! My hair was the only thing I have left that is all mine and they can't have it!

Nurses swarmed around me. I swung blindly at them, but missed every time. The masked nurse grabbed me by the waist, threw me over her shoulder, and carried me back inside the room. I kicked her stomach. She grunted in pain, but didn't let go.

She shoved me into the barber chair and buckled the straps. Dr. Vinkleman stepped in. He growled at me, "Of all the patients I've had, you've been the most troublesome, Jenna. I've decided that I'll perform a different kind of surgery on you; brain surgery."

No way is that happening! I whipped around and punched her in the eye. She stumbled backwards and knocked over bottles and syringes. Dr. Vinkleman groaned and finished the buckles. I grunted and squirmed. He laughed, "Squirm all you want. You can't escape this time. I can't wait to see what makes your brain tick."

He laughed like a mad man. I felt someone holding my hair. I felt my hair falling out. *Snip! Snip! Snip!* I cringed at every *snip!*

My hair was like my security blanket. It was my best feature, and I took pride in it. I had always washed it well and brushed it constantly. Many girls in my old school were envious of my hair, and they had always asked me if they could play with it or braid it.

I felt a razor on the back of my head. She was getting the finer hairs on my head. I will be a shiny bald person just like everyone else. Suddenly, she stopped shaving me. I felt lighter, and that feeling sickened me. I touched the blonde hairs that had fallen into my lap. This can't be happening! He laughed at me and mimicked my shocked face. He searched the drawers and pulled out a mirror.

I saw myself. I didn't look like that pretty girl back at Heidi's house. I saw a naked, bald girl. My hair was . . . gone. All that was left was shiny baldness. I could see the purple veins on the sides of my head. I looked unnatural.

I saw my reflection's eyes water. What made me tear up wasn't just my hair; it was the nurse standing behind me. The masked nurse took her mask off. It was Nurse Agnes. I felt my tired eyes widen in shock. She barely looked at me. She glanced at me quickly and then looked away. She had promised not to take my hair.

She promised . . .

I knew those kind eyes, but now they are shrouded with betrayal. She cut off my hair; my favorite thing about me. She took away my pride; my identity. She chopped off a part of me that will grow back physically, but never mentally. Why would she do this? Why didn't she resist? Even if she were put up to this, why didn't she at least put up a fight like I did?

But she . . . She promised.

Ever since I got here I've been fighting. I've fought through sickness and family and friends dying. I've watched James die in my arms. I've seen two, normal twin boys become one. I've seen the sane become insane. I've watched death happen, and I couldn't stop it.

She . . . broke her promise.

I'm not forgiving Nurse Agnes. I had trusted her! She took one of my best features away. Now only my eyes are left, and no one was getting those either. Not without a fight from me. I won't trust anyone because you never know if they'll betray you. Like Nurse Agnes or John.

I'll break her.

Nurse Agnes slowly took me out of the bonds. The look on her face told me that she's sorry, but I don't take apologies anymore. I glared at her, expressing all my anger in my face directly to her. I hope she feels as guilty as I am angry. I hope she never sleeps another night because she is so guilt ridden.

I hissed, "Traitor." She gasped quietly, but I wasn't finished. I screamed. "Agnes Felicity Holmwell, you are a traitor! You promised! You are a liar!"

She took a step back. She clutched her heart and stared wide-eyed at me. Her mouth opened and shut like a fish. I lunged at her and tried to grab her throat. Dr. Vinkleman grabbed me and yelled for soldiers. I screamed at her as I clawed for her face. I wanted to finish what I had started with that one punch.

Two soldiers walked in and grabbed my arms. I kept screaming and flailing at her, "I trusted you! James and I both! James is dead! It's your fault! All your fault! You broke your promise! Traitor! Traitor!"

James's death wasn't her fault, but I was on a ranting rampage, "He trusted you! I trusted you! You promised you wouldn't cut my hair off! I'm bald now! I trusted you! You liar! You lied!"

Tears streamed down her face. I felt them stream down mine too. Dr. Vinkleman shouted orders over my accusations. I heard nurses swarm the hallways. My ears rang, and I was still screaming, but I couldn't understand what I was saying. I don't even remember half the things I had said.

I canceled all the chaos out. I only heard one thing. Nurse Agnes opened her little mouth. She whispered one thing that still echoes in my mind. She whispered, "I'm sorry."

Chapter Twenty

I sat on the floor of my old room in the hospital. I rubbed the floor with my thumb. Kelly's blood appeared in the back of my mind. Her body flopping on the floor as she scratched her eye out. I shuddered and stood up, pulling down my short hospital gown.

If this room's walls could talk, they would tell a tale of friendship. A story about a boy and a girl who became more than just friends. All they wanted was to be free. They wanted a new life together. They wanted to be safe and sound. However, the world outside the walls was more dangerous than they had thought.

I rubbed my feet. A slightly warm cloth covered them. The nurses have been coming to my room to give me warm clothes for my feet. At first, they gave me cool ones and then slowly gave me warmer ones. My feet were slightly tingly, but it was a relief to feel them again.

What do I do now? Dr. Vinkleman will perform brain surgery on me soon. I stood up from my spot on the floor, and I walked to the door. I jiggled the doorknob, and the door was locked. I heard a growl from the other side. A dog? I heard a voice yell, "Don't even try Jew! You can't escape!"

Guards? Wow! They really want my brain. That or they don't want me to escape again. I didn't like that he told me I can't escape. Obviously I can, and I have before! That's why I'm signed up for brain surgery!

Speaking of brain surgery, how I am I going to get out of this one? Escape is always an option, but where will I escape to? The outside world was almost as dangerous as this camp. I can't hide anywhere; no one will help me, especially now since I'm completely bald. That's a dead giveaway that I'm a runaway Jew. I can't blend in without my hair.

So why should I even try to escape? Being out there was scary and dangerous. Soldiers were everywhere, and it was hard to trust anyone. I remember being in line to go into the gas chambers with the other girls. I remember thinking that I was ready to die. I wanted to just stop running and hiding. I wanted to face my fate bravely.

Should I face my fate and not prevent the surgery from happening? Giving up doesn't sound like it's the right thing to do, but sometimes the right thing to do is something you don't want to do. What if giving up is the right thing to do?

I groaned in frustration, trying to figure out my next move: to escape or to die. Where am I going to go if I escape? I can't hide anywhere, and I can't blend in anymore. Dying sounds like the right move.

I can't believe I'm thinking of dying. I've never thought of my death in depth like this. I can't believe I will die at this age by *brain surgery*. I should be making friends and learning new things at school back in Amsterdam!

I heard the guard yell at me to stop crying. He also reminded me how I will die, and I will never ever escape this room. Wow! Like I had totally forgotten that fact. Since I'll be dying anyway, I decided to toy with his temper. I shouted, "You can't contain this attitude!"

Silence came from the other side. They probably weren't used to a comeback, especially from a problem patient like me. A voice uttered. "What'd you say, Jew?"

I shot back, "I am Jewish, but I have a name just like you. My name is Jenna. I might not look so tough, but you wouldn't believe what I've been through. Your worst nightmares can't compare to my reality."

The door swung open. A tall, angry guard stomped inside my room. He shouted, "Shut up you stupid, incompetent Jew!" He kicked me down. Instead of groaning in pain, I laughed out loud. There was absolutely nothing funny about the situation I was in, but here I was dying on the floor. I was laughing so hard I couldn't breathe.

The guard was not amused. He glared at me. I stopped laughing and looked him in the eye and winked. He scowled and spat in my eye. He stormed out of the room, slammed the door behind him, and locked it.

I rubbed my eye. That was gross. My sides hurt from laughing and the bruises the guard had just given me. I really didn't know why I had laughed, but it did make him go away faster.

I examined my bruises. They weren't visible yet. I also noticed my ribs were clearly visible again. Was it lunchtime yet? I heard a knock on the door. A small voice said, "Lunch."

I didn't say anything. I knew that voice. I can't believe she had the audacity to show her face to me.

Nurse Agnes opened the door.

We stared each other down. Her right eye was blackened and bruised. That's where I punched her. I smirked at her. She walked inside the room and closed the door behind her. She stood awkwardly in front of me, looking like a scared puppy. I glared at her harder. Her eyes widened, and she looked down. I had won control. I walked to her and took the lunch tray. Today's lunch was a small sandwich and a rotten looking apple. I gave it a look of disgust, "I'm getting brain surgery, and they give me this? This certainly isn't brain food."

I chuckled at my own pun. She looked back up at me, hoping I had changed my mind about her. I stopped laughing and grimaced back at her. She quickly looked down at her shoes. I walked back to my bed to eat. I sat down and tossed my apple up in the air and caught it.

She shuffled closer to me, "Jenna."

"You can leave now," I snapped back. I caught the apple and threw it again. "Just leave me alone to die."

"No, Jenna, I'm sor—"

"Leave!" I commanded. The apple fell to the floor.

The guard ran back in and barked, "Don't use that tone with her!" he smacked me in the face. He turned around and tripped over the apple. I chuckled and Nurse Agnes smiled. He glared at both of us. "That's not funny!" He hit me in the chest. I fell back onto the bed and held my chest. He took my sandwich and left the room.

As soon as I recovered, I sat up and glared at Nurse Agnes, "Thanks, maybe I'll die of starvation before the surgery."

She had a helpless look on her face, "I'll get you another sandwich. I'm sorry."

"Sorry won't feed me, or save me," I mumbled. I picked up the apple and set it on the tray. "Please go away."

She didn't leave. She sat down next to me. I looked at her in shock. Can't she take a hint? I asked, "Why are you still here?"

She whispered, "Jenna, I want to save you. I want to help you." She moved closer to me and touched my shoulder. "I can easily get you out of here."

I growled, "And I can easily stab you with this syringe." She glanced at my hand. I had stolen her syringe from her front pocket while she was talking. I held it to her side. She gasped. I said in a soft, yet stern voice. "I don't need your help. I don't want your help. I'm not the same person anymore. I've seen too much of the outside world. There isn't a safe place for me. I'm going to face my fate . . . no matter how scary it is."

She shook her head, "You don't have to die, Jenna, I want to help you! I can keep you in my small cabin. No one goes in there but me. Please, I want to make it up to you for . . . for . . . "

Her voice trailed off. I knew what she had wanted to say. She wants to make up for cutting off my hair. I gripped the syringe and said in a low voice, "You'll never make up for what you did. Ever. I'll never forgive you."

She choked back her tears, "Please l-let me do this for you. I don't want you to d-die. P-please think about it."

"Think about it? I will die very soon! The clock is ticking!"

"You're right. Dr. Vinkleman wants to do the surgery tomorrow. He had wanted to do it right after you came, but decided not to."

I stared at her, "So I'll just stay at your little cabin forever?"

She nodded, "I'll say you're my niece visiting me. That should buy us enough time to find a way to get you out of here."

"Your bald niece?"

She sighed, "Let go of the syringe and I'll explain."

I stared at her longer, but pulled the syringe away from her side, "I'm listening."

She put her hands on the sides of her head. She slowly pulled off her hair. I gasped. Nurse Agnes wears wigs! She had a long scar on the side of her head. She explained, "When I was 17 years old, my house had caught on fire. I was upstairs in my room when it had started. I ran downstairs and tripped onto a burning rug. It had burned all of my hair off and gave me this scar. I also have some scars on my face that I cover with makeup. My hair never grew back, so I started wearing wigs."

She placed the wig on top of my head. She smiled, "It fits you well. I have some younger looking ones back in my cabin. I can get you out of here. Jenna, I'm sorry I took your hair away, but I don't want them to take your life away."

I looked down. I wanted to die. I wanted to get it over with. I was looking forward to the surgery. No more escaping and hiding. I looked back at Nurse Agnes. Her scarred, bald head gave me some hope. I touched the wig. It was nice having hair on my head again.

I felt a smile creep onto my lips. Nurse Agnes smiled too. She leaned over and hugged me, "I take that smile as a yes?"

"Yes," Suddenly, I felt myself wanting to forgive her. She's helping me again. She really cared about me, but one doubt held me back. I asked. "Nurse Agnes, why did you cut my hair?"

She pulled away from me. Her eyes went from bright and excited to dull and scared, "Jenna, I didn't want them to know I had helped you all along. I had promised you that I wouldn't cut your hair! However, Dr. Vinkleman was very suspicious of me. He even asked me if I had helped you escape. When he had asked me to cut your hair, I knew if I said no he'd throw me in jail. I'm so sorry I did it; I knew how much it meant to you."

I smiled, "I'm sorry I gave you that black eye."

She chuckled, "I think I deserved it in a way."

I looked her in the eye and said in a serious tone, because I absolutely meant it, "You didn't and I'm sorry."

She lowered her voice, "Were you telling the truth when you said James was dead?"

The name James hit me hard in the heart. His face appeared in the back of my mind. His cadaverous face with blood dripping down his cheek. His candy apple green eyes faded to a dull green. I could hear his voice whispering to me. I felt a tear slide off my cheek, "James didn't make it."

She let out a small gasp and hugged me. Her body shook in sobs. I cried with her too. We mourned James's death together. I felt better mourning with someone who cared about James too. She pulled away, "At least he is with his brother right now." I nodded. She calmed herself down and wiped the tears from her eyes. "We have to get you out of here. You ready?"

She already knew my answer.

Chapter Twenty-One

Nurse Agnes placed her wig back on her head. She took my hand and pulled me towards the door. She turned around and said quietly, "I'm sorry if I have to be mean to you."

I nodded. She grabbed me by the elbow and led me out the door. My feet stung slightly, but the longer I stood the more the pain went away. She said quickly to the guard, "I'm taking her to Dr. Vinkleman. He wants to see her."

The guard nodded. The dog growled at us. I stuck my tongue out at it. Nurse Agnes slapped me, "Don't do that! Filthy Jew!"

The slap didn't hurt too bad, but I staggered to the side just for the show. The guard nodded in approval. Nurse Agnes grabbed my hand again and led me down the hall.

The hallway was still covered in trash and feces. I saw Devin and Kevin's room. My heart lurched at the memory of them. I whispered, "What happened to Devin and Kevin?"

Nurse Agnes answered, "They died a few hours after you and James had left."

I let her words linger in my mind. Two, sweet boys who didn't deserve to die. I silently cried for them.

We passed another room. Mallory stood in the doorway. Our eyes widened at the sight of each other. Her hands were missing. She had little nubs for hands and had scars all over her arms.

My heart went out to her. She's been through just as much torture as me. Nurse Agnes noticed my gaze. She whispered, "Jenna, as much as I'd like to take every child in with me, I can't. We need to hurry."

I nodded. We had to hurry before the guard realized what was going on. Mallory whimpered my name. I tried my best to ignore her as we descended the stairs. Her whimper turned into a quiet shout. Suddenly, she was wailing my name. We hurried faster down the stairs.

Nurse Agnes said, "I'm going to scan the hallway to see if it's clear.

You wait here."

She went through a door and left me by the stairs. I could still hear Mallory's cries. Suddenly, I heard steps thumping down the stairs. Could it be nurses? I felt my heart race. I began to pace. Where could she be? Did she get dragged into something? The steps came closer and louder.

I had to leave now. I cracked open the door. No one to my left or right. Which way did she go? I slowly walked into the hallway. I noticed that this hall was much cleaner than the patient's wing. There wasn't any urine or trash on the ground. It smelled like lemons.

I heard voices, and a door opened farther down the corridor. I ducked back into the room. The thumping steps were very close now. I almost let out a shriek. I opened the door again and shut it carefully behind me. I looked to the left where the door had opened. Two nurses were walking away from me. I walked the other direction as silently and quickly as I could. I turned a corner and came face to face with Nurse Agnes. I let out a sigh of relief, "Thank goodness I found you!"

She hushed me and handed me scrubs, "Slip these on in the janitor's closet." She pointed to a door. "When you come back out, we'll head to my cabin, and I'll turn you into 'my niece'."

"Then what?"

She sighed, "We'll go from there."

That plan didn't sound too promising, but as long as it gets me out of brain surgery I'm good with it. I stepped into the janitor's closet to change. I was pulling on the shirt when I heard a few rapid knocks on the door. I almost opened the door, but someone's body slammed against it. I held in my scream.

"What are you doing, Agnes?" growled an angry voice.

"Just doing my usual duties sir," she stated in a calm voice.

"Are you a janitor now?" the voice sneered. It was definitely masculine. It sounded familiar. It hit me: John. "That's a suitable career for you."

There was silence and then footsteps. He's leaving! The door slowly cracked open. I smiled and stepped out of the closet, "That was a close one, Ag—"

I felt something crack me on my head. I fell backwards into a bucket. Waves of pain pounded against my head. I could barely focus on anything. I slowly looked up to John's grinning face, "Miss me, Jenna?"

I heard Nurse Agnes crying behind him. The last thing I saw was the butt of John's gun crashing into my head.

I woke up in a cold room. My head felt like it was split open. I touched the top of my head. Crusty, dried blood stuck to my head. I looked down at my body. I was wearing a different hospital gown, and my body was scrubbed clean. I looked around to discover I was in a surgery room. How did I get here?

Suddenly, the memories of what had happened before flooded into my aching head. I remember escaping my room with Agnes, and Mallory and nurses chasing us downstairs. It all ended with John cracking my head open with the butt of his gun. I had flickering memories of people setting me on a gurney and wheeling me through a long hallway. I remember voices and screams. I remember staring at the overhead lights and thinking I could memorize how many right and lefts we took. It was left, left, right, wait . . . no. Right, left, right, right, left . . . wait that's not it.

A door slam interrupting my thoughts. A loud laugh echoed through the room, "Jenna, Jenna, Jenna, you really thought you could escape twice? Ha-ha! You were lucky to have survived the first escape, but we caught you anyways. What made you think you could've done it again?"

Dr. Vinkleman appeared in front of me. He sneered, "I can't wait to see what virus in your brain makes you Jews act this way."

"It's not a virus! We're just like everyone else!" I protested. "I'm just like you! I'm human too! I should get the same treatment as everyone else on Earth!"

"How dare you say that I'm like you. You are inferior to me!" He shouted. He fiddled with a few controls on a machine and mumbled in German. He shouted. "Nurses! Prepare for surgery in 12 minutes!"

He left in a huff. I struggled to sit up, but the restraints covered my whole body. I shook and shimmied around to see if I could slip out of it. No luck. I took a deep breath and sighed. This was it; my last thoughts.

At least I will see James, Jacob, and all my dead friends. I'll also see Papa, Mother, and Anne. Grandma will be there! I might see Emma too. I wonder if she was dead yet. I shook my head. I can't believe I'm wondering if my sister has died.

I heard a door open. Twelve minutes had passed fast. I heard little footsteps walk towards me. That didn't sound like Dr. Vinkleman's footsteps. I turned my head to the right to see who it was. Mallory stared back at me. Maybe she can help me! I whispered, "Mallory, can you . . . oh."

Mallory held her nubs up. She couldn't help me, but how did she get here? The restraints suddenly loosened up. I looked up and saw Emma. Emma? I opened my mouth, but she quickly put a hand over it. She pressed her finger to her lips and continued to undo the restraints.

A million thoughts raced in my head. How did she get here? How did she know where I was? Did Mallory help her? Do the soldiers know she escaped? She's still alive! A tear trickled down my cheek. I'm so relieved.

Emma helped me sit up from the table. I reached my arms out to hug her, but she resisted. She spoke quickly, "We don't have much time. The nurses will be back any minute." Her voice was so thin and raspy like she hasn't had anything to drink in days.

We ran out the door with Mallory leading the way. I'm assuming Mallory helped Emma find me. How Emma got inside the hospital I haven't figured out yet.

We snuck through the hallways. No one was in the halls. We're so lucky! Mallory led us to an exit door. She pointed outside to a small cabin. Nurse Agnes's cabin! Emma pushed the door open, and we ran to the cabin. I wanted to run fast, but Emma and Mallory couldn't keep up with me. Emma was so malnourished. She panted and gasped for air. She flailed her arms to keep up with Mallory.

We finally reached the cabin. The door opened quickly when we approached it. Nurse Agnes's voice called from inside the cabin, "Hurry!"

We ran inside the cabin. Nurse Agnes shut the door and locked it behind us. Emma collapsed to the ground and gasped for air. I looked around the room. The cabin wasn't very big. We stood in a small living room. There was a brown sofa, coffee table, a rocking chair, and a door that probably led to the kitchen. There was a hallway that had three doors going down it. It was probably a bathroom and two other rooms.

Nurse Agnes led us to the kitchen. A feast had been prepared on the table. She spoon fed Emma and Mallory, and let me eat by myself. It was Emma whom she was most concerned about.

"More!" Emma protested.

"No," Nurse Agnes answered. "You can't eat too much too fast or you'll get sick. Drink more water."

Mallory opened her mouth. Nurse Agnes spooned more food inside. Mallory chewed slowly and stared at the table. I felt bad for poor Mallory. I would hate to live without my hands. She can't do much by herself.

I looked at Nurse Agnes. She still had a black eye, but her other eye looked swollen. In fact, that side of her face was very swollen. I asked, "What happened to you, Nurse Agnes?"

She glanced at me, "A soldier beat me. I'm no longer a nurse here. You can call me Agnes now."

The soldier was probably John, and he probably called her out and got her fired. I asked, "How did Em—"

Agnes said quickly, "Jenna, we'll talk later. Go help Mallory take a bath.

Take one yourself too. The bathroom is in the hallway, the first door on the right."

Emma moaned, "More please!"

Agnes nodded, "You'll get more be patient."

I looked at Mallory. She stared at me silently. I stood up and she followed me. I went down the hallway and opened the first right door. I walked into the bathroom. I walked to the tub and turned on the water. I looked at Mallory. She was struggling to take off her hospital gown. Watching her struggle made me want to cry.

I helped her out of her gown and into the bath tub. I washed her body with a bar of soap and a washcloth. She giggled in delight. She probably hasn't had a bath in who knows how long. She touched the soap bubbles with her nubs. She asked softly, "Can I stay in here for a while?"

I nodded and stepped away. I saw myself in a mirror. I couldn't believe my eyes. The blonde mass that usually covers my head and shoulders was gone. I looked like I had aged 20 years. I'm not sure if it is because of the baldness, or because in my mind I've aged.

I noticed on the counter there were toothbrushes laid out for us. There were also three blonde wigs. I touched one. It felt like real hair. Will it be the same?

I heard Mallory step out of the tub. She asked, "Can you dry me off?"

I dried her body off and wrapped the pink towel around her body. It was weird seeing her in something other than a hospital gown and a different color too. I helped her brush her teeth. I've never had to do this for someone before. When she finished rinsing her mouth out, she noticed the wigs. "Are those . . . "

I nodded, "Do you want to try one on?"

She nodded swiftly. I placed one on her head. It was a short bob. The ends of it curled slightly, framing her face. She smiled, "I like this one."

Her smile took up most of her face. She's cute when she smiles. I grinned, "It looks nice on you. Go ask Agnes for some clothes."

I opened the door for her, and she walked out of the bathroom. While the tub was filling up again, I stripped out of my hospital gown. Even though my body was scrubbed clean for the surgery, I wanted to lay in the warm water and clear my head. I stepped into the warm water and sighed with relief.

I couldn't believe I had dodged another bullet. I had escaped twice! Take that, Dr. Vinkleman! I had gotten out of brain surgery! I bet James would be proud of me.

So what will happen now? What will Agnes do with us? I really want to know how Emma escaped. Both remaining Altsmans have escaped this camp! We should get an award!

After my bath, I wrapped my body in a yellow towel. I had grabbed two towels by habit. I always use two towels; one for my body and one for my hair. I guess that's one good thing about being bald; I don't have to worry about my hair anymore, but I still miss it. I brushed my teeth and then rinsed my mouth out. My teeth felt weird being this clean.

I picked up a wig and placed it on my head. The hair went down past my shoulders. I instantly felt better having hair on my head and shoulders. I looked better too. I tried the other one on. The hair was even longer, and it had short bangs that covered my eyebrows. I like this one more.

I walked into the living room. Agnes saw me and sent Emma into the bathroom. Mallory sat on the couch wearing boy trousers and a button-down shirt. She seemed intrigued by the clothes; rubbing the fabric to her cheek. She had probably forgotten what normal clothes looked and felt like.

I sat next to her, "Do you like your clothes, Mallory?"

She nodded, "They're so soft. Those hospital gowns were so itchy!"

I chuckled, "They were itchy. I didn't like them either."

She touched her teeth, "My teeth have never felt this clean!"

I smiled, "It feels good doesn't it?"

She nodded, "I had forgotten what clean is like. This is so nice." She stroked the couch. "This couch is so soft and cushiony. I love it!"

Agnes handed me a dress and undergarments, "I think you'll fit into this. I think you're still in a woman's size. Mallory's too skinny and small. I had to put her in some boy clothes. Do you think Emma is your size?"

"I think so. I'm not sure," I answered. "Agnes, can you tell me how Emma even got here?"

She shook her head, "I think she'd rather tell you. Did you see the toothbrushes?"

I nodded. Emma came out smelling fresh. She had a big smile on her face. I almost cried. It was like looking at the old Emma, except her hair was blonde. It didn't look natural to me, but to other people I'm sure it looked fine. Agnes handed her clothes, "How was your bath?"

Emma replied, "The best bath of my life. I didn't want to leave."

She walked to a bedroom and I followed her. We changed in the room silently. The silence was killing me. I needed to talk to her! I finished putting on a white dress. It fit loosely, and it was very comfy. I looked at Emma. She wore a green dress with a gold sash around the waist. It showed off how extremely thin she was now. She had a hard time tying the sash into a bow.

"I got it," I assured her. I tied the sash. She turned around. We both stared at each other silently. I broke down first. "Oh, Emma!"

I hugged her tightly. She started to sob too. She hugged me tight and rocked from side to side. She told me how worried she was and how she had missed me. I tried to talk, but I was blubbering too much. I just stayed silent and listened to her soothing voice.

We stayed in our embrace for about ten minutes. When she was done talking, I finally was able to speak. I told her how I missed her and how happy I was that she's here now. When I was done, we both sat on the bed. Both of us were slightly exhausted from talking too much. I still had so much to ask. I asked the one question that's been bugging me since she had rescued me, "Emma, how did you get into the hospital?"

She explained, "When I saw you by the barracks yesterday, I couldn't believe it. It had felt like months since I last saw you. I guess a soldier noticed me staring and asked me if I was related to you. I had to answer so I told him I was your sister. I guess he had told a doctor, and then the doctor wanted to see me. I was sent to the hospital and put in a room next to that girl out there. Her name is Mallory right?"

I nodded. She continued telling me how Mallory helped her find me. I hugged her again and told her my unbelievable tales. When I finished, she hugged me and whispered, "Papa would be so proud of you, Jenna. You were much stronger and braver than me."

Her saying that made my heart fill with joy. Through all the hardships I've experienced, this little moment of happiness pushed them all away.

We walked back to the living room. Mallory was drinking a soda from a straw. The soda sat on a coaster on the coffee table. She would lean to the soda and sip out of the straw. Every sip she took she'd stop and giggle. Agnes watched her and chuckled to herself. She smiled at us, "Mallory told me that she's never had a soda before."

Mallory sipped again and laughed louder, "This tastes amazing! I never thought I'd get to drink one of these!"

We all smiled and laughed. I had never seen Mallory so excited about something so small like a soda. Her whole face glowed, and her eyes had a happy glint to them. She almost looked like a normal, little girl for a moment.

Agnes gestured Emma and I to the kitchen. We sat down at the little table. Agnes explained, "We don't have much time, girls. They're probably searching the whole camp for all of you right now."

Emma nodded, her serious, focused face taking place, "How are we getting out of here?"

Agnes shook her head, "I don't know. I wish I could send you girls on a truck out of here, but I'm sure Jenna knows how dangerous it is out there."

I agreed, "Very dangerous."

Agnes said, "I have an idea. Since I'm fired, I have to leave the camp. I thought about going to America and starting a new life there. There's a boat that leaves from The Hague to go there."

Emma smiled, "Our grandparents live there. It's by the coast in the Netherlands."

Agnes said, "I can get papers for all of us from an old friend of mine. Do you girls want to come with me?"

Emma and I looked at each other. We both knew what the other was thinking. Emma beamed, "Yes!"

Agnes smiled, "Great! You two should look fine wearing my blonde wigs. There is a problem though."

I asked, "What?"

Agnes lowered her voice, "Mallory."

Emma raised an eyebrow, "What about her?"

Agnes said, "Well . . . she doesn't have hands. Some eyebrows will be raised and questions will be asked if she's out in public."

Emma stood up and paced. She always did that when she thinks, "If we gave her a big coat that covered her hands she'd be fine!"

Agnes nodded, "But what if they needed to see her hands for some reason? Or what if one of her sleeves accidently slides up and they see?"

"So we leave her here?" I shouted. "We're not doing that!"

Agnes groaned, "I know! I don't want to leave her here either, but I don't know what to do!"

"Maybe no one will notice!" I snapped.

Emma exclaimed, "We could put gloves on her! If they're snug on the wrist, they won't fall off!"

Agnes got up and searched a cabinet. She pulled out a bag of gloves. She explained, "These are my gloves. I think I still have a small pair that I had worn when I was very young."

They were in a variety of sizes. She searched until she pulled out a pair of very small gloves. Emma and I cheered. Agnes said seriously, "We need to leave now."

Chapter Twenty-Two

Agnes quickly packed each of us a change of clothes in a bag. Mallory looked out the window and watched for any signs of soldiers. Emma and I talked together in the kitchen.

"Mother was a mess," Emma told me. "With Papa and Anne dead and then you were taken away, she couldn't function at all. We were both assigned to cleaning the soldiers' homes. Mother couldn't clean. She would try to sweep a floor, but then she'd break down and cry! I didn't want the soldiers to beat her to death, so I did her work for her."

"Did you get caught?" I asked.

Emma nodded, tears forming in her eyes, "Yes. I did. A young soldier had come into the room. Mother was sitting on the floor, and I was cleaning. He had asked her why she wasn't working. She didn't answer fast enough so he slapped her. I had stepped in and said I was doing my work and hers. He said I'm not supposed to do that, and Mother will be punished. I told him I would take her punishment."

She paused and wiped tears from her eyes. I asked, "Did he beat you?"

"No," she answered solemnly. "He said if I had sex with him, he wouldn't tell. I also couldn't tell anyone that I did it with him."

Her words hit me hard in the heart. Emma always swore she would only have sex when she was married. It must have been a hard thing for her to do. She cried softly, "I didn't want Mother to die."

I hugged her and let her cry on my shoulder, "At least it was only once right?"

She suddenly pulled away and cried, "That's not even half of it, Jenna! They barely fed us anything! All we got was watery soup. Mother was losing her strength, and she couldn't even walk because she was so weak and hungry. The soldier had come again and told me he could give me extra food in exchange for sex, and I couldn't tell anyone. I agreed to it. He would take me to his cabin at night and then escort me to the barracks after we were done. The next day while we were working, he would come in and hand me a loaf of bread and water. I gave it to Mother every time. Papa would be so ashamed of me. I'm ashamed of myself."

She let out a soft wail. I hugged her, "Don't be ashamed. You helped Mother for as long as you could."

She smiled softly. Agnes came into the kitchen, "We need to leave now."

Mallory called from the living room, "I see them! I see soldiers!" She ran to the kitchen. "They're carrying big guns! They're headed this way!"

Agnes said hastily, "Run out the back door. I have my truck parked out there. All of our supplies are in there. Go!"

Emma, Mallory, and I ran out the back door. I opened the truck door and helped Mallory get in the truck. I called to Emma, "Where's Agnes?"

Emma turned around and looked at the back door, "I don't see her. She's not coming!"

"What?" I asked. "She has to drive, she's the one with the plan!" I made Emma help Mallory. I ran back to the cabin. I saw the soldiers step inside the cabin. I ducked behind a trash can while Agnes talked to the soldiers.

"Girls? What girls?" She asked with a look of innocence on her face.

"You know well enough!" shouted a soldier. I think it was John. "You've been helping them all along! Now, where are they?"

Agnes shrugged, "I know nothing. I'm packing right now. I haven't seen any girls running around outside my cabin. Perhaps they've already escaped."

John growled and raised a hand. Agnes flinched and moved back. John laughed, "If you are so sure you haven't seen them, you wouldn't mind us searching your cabin?"

Agnes snapped, "I'm not hiding those girls! You can leave right now!"

John pushed her aside, "Search the cabin!"

John and the soldiers went to the bedrooms. I stood up and waved at Agnes. She glanced over at me and motioned for me to go back. I didn't move away. I won't leave without her. I walked confidently to her. Her eyes widened in terror. She moved towards me and pushed me out the back door. She hissed, "What are you doing? You can't just strut in here! The soldiers would have seen you!"

"We're not leaving without you!" I hissed back. "We need you to drive the truck."

"The soldiers are here. I can't leave!"

"Agnes, we can go now! Let's leave now while they don't know!"

"Jenna—"

Suddenly, a gunshot pierced my ears. They started to ring. I fell backwards in surprise. Agnes's eyes widened. She fell to her knees. Her chest was red. I heard a scream and realized it was coming from me.

I saw John standing behind her. He held a smoking pistol. He reloaded it and glared directly at me. I'm a goner. Suddenly, I felt hands wrap around my waist and pull me to my feet. I thought it was a soldier so I tried to resist. I turned around to see Emma. She took my hand, and we ran to the truck. I heard a gun fire, and a bullet whizzed by my ear. I heard John shouting at the soldiers.

Emma climbed into the driver's side while I jumped into the passenger side. She whispered, "Agnes."

I held her tight. I said, "It's ok, Mallory. Emma, start the truck!"

"It won't turn on! Wait . . . now I remember!" She pushed down on one of the pedals and turned the key. The truck roared to life. She said. "Hey, Jenna?"

"Yes?"

"I don't know how to drive."

"Oh . . . wait what?"

She suddenly gunned the truck. It lurched forward and then died. I yelled, "Why did you turn it off?"

"I didn't mean to! I've got to get used to this!" she yelled back. "Be patient!"

"Well, we haven't got all day, they are coming after us!" I shouted.

"Don't yell at me!" she snapped.

The truck gunned forward again, and we started bouncing along the road. I heard gunshots fire behind us. I turned around. The soldiers had finally caught up to us. I yelled, "Why didn't you tell me you couldn't drive?"

"Papa taught me a little, but then the car was damaged and we couldn't practice anymore. Don't you remember?" she looked at me. "You and Anne were upset because—"

I yelled, "Watch where you're going! Look out!"

She swerved, barely missing a fencepost, "No need to yell!"

I yelled louder, "Drive to the gate! Turn here!" She cranked the wheel around . . . the wrong way. I shouted hysterically. "What do you think you're doing?"

"Well, you didn't say which direction!" she retorted. "You need to be more specific!"

"Turn left! Left was the only direction to go! You couldn't turn right there because the road didn't go that way! Geez! I might as well ask Mallory to drive!"

Emma glared at me. I heard Mallory laugh a little. I'm glad I'm brightening up the mood. We drove past soldiers who didn't even notice us. I'm surprised they didn't pull us over because of how reckless Emma was driving. Unfortunately, as we passed them, they noticed the angry band of soldiers chasing after us and realized their mistake. Mallory turned around, "Uh oh."

"What is it?" I asked. I turned around. Two trucks followed behind us. John was in the first one. He leaned out the window and fired at us. He hit the right side mirror. The glass shattered and we all screamed.

"I can see the gate! It's open!" cried Mallory. "Drive faster! We can make it!"

A shot blasted the other side mirror. We all jumped again. Emma sobbed, "Oh no! It's closing!"

Soldiers scattered around the gates, trying to shut it before we got to it. I yelled, "Emma, drive faster!"

Emma slammed on a pedal. The truck came to a sudden stop and we were flung forward. I grunted, "Wrong pedal!"

"Sorry!" she exclaimed. She pushed a different one. The truck sped up. We still weren't going fast enough. She cried, "This is as fast as it will go!"

I looked at the speedometer. We were barely going 20 mph.

Mallory said softly, "You need to switch gears."

Emma and I looked at her, "Huh?"

Mallory explained, "Push down the far left pedal and then move that stick."

Emma followed her instructions. She moved the stick and hit the gas pedal. The truck moved faster. I saw soldiers carrying spikes. I screamed, "They're going to pop the wheels! Faster!!"

Emma pushed down harder on the gas pedal. Just before the soldiers threw the spikes in our path, we zipped past the closing gates. I turned around. The soldiers were furiously trying to reopen the gates. I think the gate was broken. I gave Mallory a look of awe, "How do you know about cars?"

She explained, "I used to watch my daddy drive. I don't really know how it works though. I just remember how he did things like switching gears."

I smiled, "Well, it's a good thing we have you with us! We wouldn't have made it without you!"

Mallory beamed back at me. I bet she feels good knowing that she's helpful to us, even though she doesn't have hands.

"We aren't free yet. Where are we going?" asked Emma nervously. She switched gears, and the truck moved faster. "They won't stay behind those gates for long."

"Is there a map in here we can use?" I asked.

Mallory sat up, "I think I'm sitting on it!"

She lifted her butt up, and I pulled out a map from underneath her. As I studied it, I saw that Agnes drew a line on the road we needed to go on. We were in the middle of Germany. The map didn't say where, Agnes just had a circle around a small area. The line went out to the coast of Netherlands. There was a circle around The Hague.

A memory of summer vacations came to my mind. We had gone to The Hague to see my grandparents. It had rained the whole time we were there, but my grandparents made it fun. Grandma had baked cookies and grandpa told stories. Grandma had shown me old photo albums of when she was my age. We looked so much alike!

"Ok, Emma, turn *right* here," I commanded. "We'll be on this road for a while.

Mallory asked, "What if they're tracking us? It's no use escaping if we're basically making tracks for them to follow."

Emma agreed, "Mallory is right. We need to cover our tracks."

She pulled the truck over. We got out and examined the snowy road. You could clearly see the tire tracks. Mallory said, "We need something to cover those up."

I looked in the bed of the truck. Our bags were in there and a big bag of food with a lot of money in it. I handed Emma the food bag, "Keep that inside; we can eat that along the way." I couldn't find anything else that could help mask our tracks.

"It's starting to snow again," Emma observed. "The new fallen snow will cover the tracks, and if we hurry, we can get on another road that already has tracks on it."

We all piled in the truck again and continued down the road. I looked through the food bag. Agnes had packed fruits, dried meat, and little bottles full of water. I also found a stash of cash. It was enough to pay for all of us to go to America.

We traveled to a fork in the road. The map said we had to turn right. The right road had tire tracks on it. I cheered, "There are other tracks! Now, they can't follow us!"

Emma said, "Hold on." She turned the truck left.

"Emma, what are you doing?" I asked. "You turned the wrong way again."

"I'm going to trick them," she said. She drove for a little bit and then put the truck in reverse. We drove backwards until we returned to the fork.

Emma turned right and continued on the correct road. She explained. "They'll see both tracks and get confused. It'll buy us more time."

The sky grew darker as we drove along the snowy road. Emma had to switch with me because she became tired. She showed me how to work the clutch and shift gears. It took me a few tries to get it right.

After driving for a few hours, I felt my eyes droop slightly, but I had to stay alert. Mallory was still awake, so I decided to ask her about her family. I said casually, "So, Mallory, what's your family like? Are any of them still alive?"

Mallory shook her head, "Well, I'm Jewish like you. Daddy died on the train. Mommy died in the gas chamber. My older sister, Heather, is in the camp, so maybe she's still alive. I don't know if you know this, but I killed my twin, Annabelle, at the hospital."

I remembered back in the cafeteria when Kristen and Kelly told me why Mallory went crazy. Mallory, as if she were reading my mind, said, "I'm not as crazy as you think. The pills and shots are what drove me insane. I feel better now that I haven't been stabbed with a needle in a while."

"Why did you kill Annabelle?" I asked. "I know she got more attention than you, but she's your sister!"

Mallory sighed, "I know. I regret it so much. Before I did it, I had hated her so much. Dr. Vinkleman had absolutely loved her. I couldn't stand her being so happy all the time while I was getting so sick. After I . . . did it, I realized how much I needed Annabelle. Even though I hated her, she had truly brought out the best in me. No wonder Dr. Vinkleman had liked her more than me. Same with my parents; they had always adored her, and Heather did too. I didn't get much attention. I had gotten so sick of it that . . . I just . . . anger took control of me and . . . ." Her voice trailed off.

I said softly, "I'm sorry. In a way, I know how you feel. My younger sister Anne got a lot of attention and so did Emma. I'm the middle child. I got some attention, but not as much as them. My grandma really cared about me. We were so similar. I feel like she was my twin in a way."

We were silent. Mallory finally spoke, "I used to have a friend in the hospital. Her name was Selene. She was the only person who had ever paid attention to me. She reminds me of you."

I smiled, "How?"

"She was nice to me and listened to me," she said softly. "She died from drinking too much seawater."

"Why did she do that?" I asked.

She looked down sadly, "She didn't decide it. Dr. Vinkleman had decided to do that. He wouldn't let her eat. He had made her drink only seawater. Suddenly, she wasn't herself anymore. All she cared about was finding water and food. I had sometimes snuck an apple to her so she could eat it and have its juice, but it was no good. I found her trying to lick the hallway floor after a nurse had mopped it. She had drunk toilet water and got even sicker after that. She didn't survive very long. She was the only person I really saw as . . . family in that horrible place."

My eyes were almost shut by the time dawn came. I struggled to drive straight. Emma woke up and looked out the window, "Jenna! Stop the truck!"

I stopped the truck and looked around, "What's wrong?"

"Turn the engine off!" she hissed.

I turned it off and looked out her window. I saw snow-covered trees and bushes. On the other side of the forest, there was a snow covered path. Shivering people in striped rags walked along the path. Soldiers carried guns and followed them. I gasped. It was another death march.

Emma whispered, "We'll wait until they've passed. Hopefully, they won't see us through the thick brush."

It took a while for them to pass. It was hard to watch the stumbling bald people walk. It was even harder to watch the soldiers shoot the fallen people. A man had attempted to run away. He had made it to the ditch before he was shot. I heard Emma sniffling and wiping tears away. Poor Mallory used her stubs to wipe them from her cheek.

"Why would they do this?" Emma cried. "Why would they do this to normal people? Innocent people?"

I wish I knew the answer to that question.

Emma kept watch on the death marchers while Mallory and I were sleeping. When we woke up, they were still marching. I looked behind us. Our tracks were completely covered by snow, and the hood of the truck was covered too. I asked, "How long have we been asleep Emma?"

"Only a few hours," she reported. "Look over there, I see the last of them!"

I looked toward the people marching, and I could see few soldiers walking behind the group of marchers. They were the last people. We waited until they were completely out of sight. I turned on the engine. It groaned and sputtered.

Emma said, "I don't think you're not starting the truck right!"

"I'm doing it right!" I argued. "You couldn't even steer it! Mallory, what do you think is wrong?"

Mallory shrugged, "I know how to drive a car, but I don't know a thing about what's under the hood."

Emma suggested, "Maybe the snow is making the engine cold."

"That is the stupidest thing I've ever heard," I laughed.

"Well, it might work," Mallory said. "Just brush the snow off the hood. I've seen my dad do that before."

We had nothing to lose. Emma and I got out of the truck and brushed the snow off the hood. It took a while to brush off the cold, compacted snow. We climbed back into the truck.

I shivered and said, "This b-better w-w-work!"

Emma's teeth chattered, "T-t-t-try it n-n-n-now."

My shaky hands turned the key. The engine sputtered to life. Mallory cheered, "It worked! To The Hague!"

"To The Hague!" Emma and I echoed her gleefully. I put the truck in gear, and we sped off through the snow.

Chapter Twenty-Three

We passed towns full of little shops and homes. We stopped once at noon to eat and filled the truck up with gas. Mallory wanted to explore all the shops and towns, but we didn't have time. We didn't know if the soldiers or the whole Nazi Party was looking for us. We had to keep moving until we arrive in America.

Maybe we could get to America by Hanukah, and Emma, Mallory, and I could celebrate it together. Hanukah will be difficult this year. I'm used to celebrating it with family. Now, the only family I have left is Emma . . . and Mallory. I guess she counts.

Agnes popped into my mind. I haven't thought much about her. I think it's because I've been so focused on other things. Her death was so sudden, and we haven't had the time to properly mourn it. We haven't had funerals for any of our family members either.

I pulled the truck over. Emma asked, "Are you tired, Jenna? Do you want to switch?"

I shook my head, "No, I'm fine. I've been thinking about Agnes. We haven't had a proper funeral for her, or for Anne, or Mother, or Papa."

"Annabelle and Selene," whispered Mallory.

"Yes, but we need to keep moving," urged Emma. "We can have a nice funeral for everyone when we don't have to run anymore."

"No, we should do this now while we're still in Europe," I insisted. "It won't take long. Can we do a short prayer?"

We stayed in the truck. Emma said, "Ok, bow your heads. I think each of us should say a short prayer. Mallory, you first."

Mallory cleared her throat, "Lord, please take care of my parents and my sisters. Tell Annabelle I'm sorry for what I did. I am sorry, Annabelle. Also, take care of Selene. Let her know how much her company meant to me."

I said, "Please look after my parents and my little sister. Let them know how much I love them. Take care of James and Jacob, Devin and Kevin, and Kristen and Kelly. Watch over all the children in the hospital and the concentration camps."

Emma finished, "And please take care of Agnes. We wouldn't have made it this far without her help. Amen."

We all hugged each other and sat silently for a few minutes. I started the truck and continued driving. I feel like all the sadness and burden has been lifted off my shoulders. The tension in the truck lifted as well. Mallory had a smile on her face, and Emma wasn't as tense as before. I feel much better too.

We arrived at The Hague around noon. I drove to the marina and parked the truck. We walked to the boardwalk. There were many shops and booths along the boardwalk. We used a small amount of money to buy sweet bread and water. We split the loaf and ate on a bench.

Mallory was wearing the coat with long sleeves and gloves. I fed her small pieces of bread when no one was looking. It didn't matter, people did stare at us. I don't think it was because they saw Mallory's nubs. I think it was how sick and thin we looked. Our clothes were baggy, and our faces were emaciated. They didn't point at us or make us feel like we were some show at a circus, we just got long, concerned stares.

I was ecstatic to be away from the hospital. I missed the city life; the sound of cars and people. It seemed brighter and happier here. People walked with each other, and no one was beaten or murdered. People had conversations without getting upset and no one was being beaten. No one was starving or horribly sick. Everyone was unique and different, and people were fine with it.

Then there's me. What is so wrong with me? I'm just a Jewish girl.

We searched for a place that sold tickets to get on the boat. We wandered along the shops and stores that sold candies and clothes and toys. Mallory was nostalgic. She wanted to touch and try everything. Emma said no every time she asked for something. I think Emma pretends Mallory is Anne sometimes. Emma usually said no to Anne, but if Anne asked me I usually said yes.

Mallory did ask me several times, but I had to say no. I wanted to say yes, but we had to leave as soon as possible. If the soldiers find us, we're dead. Emma exclaimed, "I see a ticket booth over there."

We rushed to the booth. An old man smiled, "What can I do for you young ladies?"

"Hi, we need three tickets for the next boat to America please!" Emma requested. She pulled out some of the money Agnes had given us. "I think this should be enough."

He counted the money and smiled, "That's just enough, but how old are you? I also need to see some papers."

Agnes was supposed to get us papers. Emma glanced at me, "Um . . . we don't have any."

"Where are your parents?" he asked.

They're both dead! I thought quickly and said, "They're in America. They only had enough money to send themselves. They got jobs, and they finally sent enough money for us to go!"

He sat back, eyebrows raised, "Oh, really? Who have you been staying with this whole time, miss?"

"They've been with me, sir," a familiar voice said. I froze. I knew the voice. I slowly turned around. John smiled down at me. He put his arm on my shoulder, and I tensed up. He continued. "I'm their uncle, sir."

He's still wearing his uniform. I'm shocked that he found us. How did he find us? The old man nodded, "I see. They were about to buy tickets to America."

John shook his head, "We're not doing that today. I'm sorry to have wasted your time, sir. Come along, girls."

He grabbed Emma's hand and pushed my back forcefully. I looked back at Mallory. She followed us with a terrified look on her face. John spoke calmly, "I didn't think I'd find you girls, but here you are! Aren't you glad I found you?"

Emma growled, "Let us go!"

He chuckled and led us to a truck, "If you're lucky, I'll let all of you go into a gas chamber where you belong and that's if you're lucky."

The truck was similar to the one that had transported my family to the train station. If we get in that truck, there's no turning back. I mumbled very quietly to Emma, "When I run, grab Mallory and run."

I saw her nod slightly. I shot forward quickly. John couldn't grab my shoulder quick enough. I looked over my shoulder to check if Emma and Mallory had caught on. Emma carried Mallory, and they headed the opposite direction. John yelled at the soldiers in the truck to catch us. I circled around to catch up to Emma and Mallory.

The soldiers were out of the truck and running towards us. John was in the lead. I finally caught up to Emma. I noticed her wig was missing. She cradled Mallory in her arms. She panted, "John . . . tried to . . . grab my hair . . . and . . . he took off . . . the wig."

I took Mallory from her so her arms could rest. We dashed through the crowd. The soldiers shouted for the crowd to part. We still had a big lead, but we had to buy the tickets. We slammed into the ticket booth.

The old man yelled, "Hey! Don't hit my booth! Oh, it's you. Why are you here again?"

I set Mallory on the ground. I leaned close to the old man's face and said in a low voice, "We need tickets. Now."

He laughed, "Girls, quit trying! Not only has the boat already left for America, but you can't buy a ticket *anywhere* without papers."

I heard whistles and shouts behind us. John's voice rose above them all. We took off running. Hearing his voice brought me back to when I was in the village. He had beaten me senseless and so did most of the villagers. I shuddered at the memory. I don't want it to happen again.

I pumped my arms and legs faster. Emma panted trying to keep up with me. I heard someone cry out my name. I looked over my shoulder. Mallory had fallen down and couldn't get up. I skidded to a stop and turned around. Emma called back to me, "Jenna! No!"

I ran to Mallory. A soldier was running to us. I beat him to her and quickly helped her stand up. As soon as she fully stood up, a club came swiftly down on her. I tripped and fell backwards. The image of the hammer swinging onto Anne came to my mind. The soldier raised the club into the air. I screamed and tried to pull Mallory's bloody body away, but someone grabbed me by my waist and dragged me away.

I heard Emma say, "Jenna, get on your feet! We have to run! There are more soldiers coming!"

I stood up and ran with her. I didn't want to run. I wanted to save Mallory, but I couldn't save her. I looked over my shoulder.

Mallory howled and tried to crawl away from the soldier. Every time she struggled to stand up she was beaten down. More soldiers came and beat her with their clubs. Her bald head was red with blood. Her bloody and dirty wig laid on the ground.

We ran about 100 feet away from the scene. I heard a sing-song voice call, "Clara Oh, Clara, turn around!"

I grabbed Emma's hand and made her stop. I turned around and saw John. I stared at him, and he glared at me. His twisted, angry face made me feel sick. I noticed he wasn't sending the soldiers to get us. All of the soldiers were beating Mallory. He was doing this to make us mad. He wanted me to turn around and watch.

Emma tugged my hand, "He's doing this to make you mad. We have to keep going!"

"I know," I answered.

He smirked and dramatically raised his pistol high in the air. He lowered it and pointed it at Mallory's head. Emma hissed, "He might point it at us next!" The soldiers stepped away from Mallory. She whimpered softly on the ground. Emma tried to pull me away. "It's a trap! He'll send the soldiers to us! Let's go, Jenna!"

I didn't move. I stood still and watched.

He fired.

I flinched.

People who were watching didn't do a thing. They didn't intervene, or protest. All they did was watch the bloody spectacle taking place. They thought it was a show. I thought I heard a few people applauding.

Emma yanked my arm, "Jenna!"

Suddenly, John pointed the gun at Emma and fired.

Chapter Twenty-Four

I stared at Emma in shock. Her eyes widened, but she didn't fall over or scream in pain. I didn't see any blood on her either. I wanted to ask if she was ok, but she quickly grabbed my hand and took off into a run.

I heard John tell the soldiers to catch us. We ran down the whole boardwalk. People moved away from us when we ran. It was as if they were scared to even touch us!

Emma led me into a small alleyway by a restaurant. She pulled me behind a trash can. She plopped to the floor. She was breathing hard. I sat next to her and asked, "Emma, are you alright?"

She snapped, "Jenna, I almost died back there. I told you it was a trap! You should've listened to me!"

I said softly, "I'm sorry. Are you ok?"

"I could hear the bullet fly by my right ear! It was terrifying, but I'm fine," she said. I sighed in relief. She stared at the other garbage cans. It smelled so bad. She asked, "Are you ok?"

I shook my head, "Mallory."

Emma hugged me, "It'll be alright. She's in a place where no one can hurt here anymore. She's happier now."

Mallory helped us so much. If it wasn't for her, we wouldn't have made it out of that camp alive. She was so defenseless; she didn't have hands! Maybe someday the world we live in will be better for people like Mallory.

I heard a low voice ask, "Are you ok?"

"Emma, I told you I'm fine!" I said.

"I didn't repeat myself," Emma said slowly.

We looked to where the voice was coming from. A man in dark clothes stared at us. We both shrieked and stood up to run. He said softly, "Wait! I'm not going to hurt you."

Emma snapped, "Oh, sure you won't!"

Suddenly, I heard whistles and shouts. They were catching up to us. We crouched behind the trash cans. I asked, "Emma, what do we do?"

He said with a look of sincerity on his face, "I want to help you."

"We can't trust anyone!" Emma hissed. "Let's hide in the trash cans, Jenna. They wouldn't stop to look there."

"I saw what had happened to you. I saw the soldier kill your friend. I'm from a secret resistance. I help Jewish refugees escape!" he pleaded. "Let me help you."

Papa had talked about the resistance. He only talked about them to Mother when we were asleep, but I could still hear them. He had wanted to ask for help from one, but I guess it was too late. I grabbed Emma's hand, "Wait, Emma, I remember Papa talking about people like him."

He asked, "What's your Papa's name?"

"Charles Altsman," Emma answered.

"I remember him. He had contacted me, and I answered him, but he never replied back. Is your mother's name Mary?"

"Yes!" I said excitedly. "Emma, we should trust him!"

Emma looked unsure. The whistles and shouts grew louder. The man coaxed, "I would never hurt you, only help you."

"Ok," Emma said reluctantly. We really didn't have a choice.

The man opened a door and led us inside the restaurant. We walked through the kitchen area. New smells and sounds danced in the air. He led us to a small table in the kitchen. He instructed us to stay there.

We sat down at the table. A chef brought us sandwiches. I had forgotten what pastrami and cheese tasted like. The cheese was so warm and gooey. We drank fresh milk to wash it down.

The man came back, "Were the sandwiches tasty?"

We nodded and thanked him. I got a better look at him. He was very tall and had dirty blonde hair and blue eyes. His German accent was heavy, but he spoke Dutch very well. He wore a black suit and matching hat.

He led us to a small stairwell. We climbed up the stairs and into a small apartment. He gestured for us to sit down. He walked to the kitchen and came back with glasses of water. We took the water and drank it greedily. I didn't realize how thirsty I was. He asked, "So how did you girls escape?"

I explained our whole escape up to this point. He nodded, "Did you say the nurse's name was Agnes?"

We nodded, "Yes, she died helping us."

He looked down sorrowfully, "That's a shame. You see, I'm the old friend she was referring to. We were good friends when I lived close to her. She did a lot of favors for me, and I owe her."

"She helped us a lot too," Emma commented. "She gave us clothes, money, and a ride here."

He smiled, "She was very nice. I want to make it up to her. I would love to help you girls get to safety."

Emma grinned at me. I smiled back, "So you'll help us?"

"Of course, any friend of Agnes is a friend of mine," he smiled. "Where would you like to go? I could forge papers for both of you and get you tickets."

Emma and I both answered, "America!"

He shook his head, "America is tricky. Not everyone gets accepted there. There are so many other places you can go. Switzerland would be your best option. There are many trains going there."

"Well, when can we leave?" Emma asked. "We need to leave here as soon as possible."

He frowned slightly, "Well, it's hard to get papers forged these days because of the demand for them. Ticket prices have gone up as well. It may take a few weeks to get the money to pay for all of it."

Emma offered, "We have money! We also have a truck you can sell for more money! We'll pay you!"

He lit up, "Really? That would definitely speed up the process! I might be able to get your papers ready by tomorrow."

Emma looked at me. I nodded in approval. She stood and shook his hand, "It's a deal!"

He smiled, "Great! I'll also provide you with clothes. You need some warm ones to live by the Alps."

While Emma paid him, I asked, "What's your name?"

He answered, "Cecil Farris. I will tell my wife to get some nice clothes for you two."

"Thank you so much, Mr. Farris," Emma said. She handed him the keys to the truck.

He smiled, "Call me Cecil. What are your names?"

"I'm Emma and she's my sister, Jenna," Emma said.

"Didn't you have another sister? A little one named Anne?" he asked.

I looked down sadly. Emma patted my back, "She didn't make it. Neither did our parents."

"Oh, I'm so sorry," he said apologetically. "I shouldn't have asked that."

Emma smiled sadly, "It's fine, Cecil."

"I'm terribly sorry for your losses. Well, girls, make yourself at home. My wife, Minerva, should be home soon. Help yourself to anything in the kitchen," he tipped his hat to us and went downstairs.

Emma and I immediately crashed on the couch. We were both extremely exhausted. It didn't take long for me to fall asleep.

"Hello?" asked a tiny, squeaky voice. I cracked open an eye. Huge, blue eyes stared at me. A long, red fingernail poked my nose. "Are you awake, girl?"

I sat up slowly. I came face to face with a lady. If I'm face to face with someone while I'm sitting on the couch, they must be very small. I stood up. Her doll-like face barely came to my chest. I'm a small person, but this lady was very, very small.

"Yes! I'm very small! There's no need to stare!" she snapped. Her squeaky voice made me want to laugh. Her eyes were too big and her mouth was too small. Her hair was blonde and went to her chin. "You have no manners! It's not polite to stare!"

"Sorry, I—"

"Here, try this on!" she handed me red thermal underwear. I looked at Emma's couch. She wasn't there. The lady squeaked. "Your sister is in the bathroom changing."

Emma walked out of the bathroom. She had on a puffy coat and baggy pants. A warm looking hat covered her head. She tripped in her clunky boots. She was sweating, "It's very warm."

"Well, you'll need warm clothes living in the Alps!" the lady pushed me towards the bathroom. "You go try those on."

I tried on the same outfit as Emma's. I was also sweating as I walked out of the bathroom. The lady nodded in approval, "Those look fine."

Cecil opened the door, "Good news!"

"Hello, darling," the lady stood on her tiptoes. Cecil bent down and let her kiss him. Cecil smiled and asked, "I see you gave the girls clothes, Minerva?"

She nodded, "Nice, warm ones."

"Good! I have great news, girls," he set two papers down on the table. "I've got your papers finished! I sold the truck to a friend of mine, and that money bought the papers."

Emma and I waddled to the table and picked up the papers. I read mine out loud, "Jenna Beth Hoven, 17 years old, Religion—Protestant. Born in Munich, Germany. October 7, 1919."

Emma read, "Emma Marie Hoven, 18 years old, Religion—Protestant. Born in Munich, Germany. November 13, 1918."

"I know those aren't your real birthdays or religion, but I had to change your whole identity. I kept your first names though." Cecil explained.

Emma smiled, "Perfect! These are great! Thank you, Cecil."

Cecil beamed and asked, "Minerva, dear, will you make dinner? I must go to the train station and buy their tickets for Switzerland."

Minerva nodded, "That's fine, darling."

Cecil grabbed our papers and left quickly. Emma and I changed back into our old clothes and helped Minerva cook dinner. We set the table and ate quietly. I asked, "So how long have you and Cecil been doing this?"

"Not very long," she said. "About a year. I like doing it though. I like helping people. I don't believe in Hitler's ways."

"What made you want to do it?" I asked.

"A year and a half ago, a girl was beaten outside our restaurant. She was about 14 years old, a skinny little thing. She was begging for food outside. I had told Cecil to grab some bread to give to her. I had turned my back for a minute, and the Gestapo attacked the poor girl. They had beaten her with sticks and threw her in a trash can. She was so skinny and small she fit inside perfectly. They had thrown the trash can in the alleyway and left." She shook her head. "The poor girl's blood had stained the inside of the can. We had taken her inside the apartment and tried to nurse her back to health, but she died later that day."

"That's awful," Emma commented. "What was her name?"

"Helena. Helena Cromwell," Minerva said. "Her father used to be a wealthy banker. He was sent to a death camp. When the Gestapo had come for Helena, her mother hid her under the floorboards of their house. The Gestapo had asked where she was, but her mother refused to tell. They had taken her mother instead and left the house. Helena had lived on the streets for months."

"Helena?" Emma gasped. "I had gone to school with her until we switched schools," Emma gasped. "We were good friends."

"I'm sorry, love. She was a sweet girl," She patted Emma's back. Emma nodded and wiped a few tears from her eyes. Minerva announced. "I have more clothes for you girls to try on."

We tried on more clothes; dresses, thermal underwear, boots, hats, gloves, coats, big coats, and socks. When we were done, Minerva played music on her record player, and we danced around the apartment. It was the most fun I've had in a while. While Emma took a bath, I packed some of our clothes into the suitcases. Minerva said, "I noticed you're wearing a wig."

I nodded, "Yes. They had shaved both of our heads at the camp. Emma lost her wig when we were running away from the soldiers."

Minerva assured, "Don't worry. Your hair will grow back soon."

"I hope so," I answered.

Emma walked in wearing a towel. Minerva handed her a green nightgown. I went to the bathroom and took off my clothes. I looked in the mirror and took off my wig. The veins in my head popped out. I touched them. The skin felt soft and smooth. It felt so weird. I'm use to touching soft hair, not skin.

I turned on the water and stepped inside the tub. The warm water felt amazing on my skin. I wanted to stay in the tub forever. I slowly washed my body. When I was finally done, I got out of the tub and dried off with a towel. I glanced at my wig. My hair had always been my identity, but that wig wasn't my hair. My bald head is my new identity. Why should I cover up who I am anymore? I tossed it in the trashcan.

I walked out in my towel. Minerva handed me a lacy nightgown. I gasped. It looked like my old nightgown. Minerva asked, "Is something wrong?"

"I'm fine thank you," I smiled and took the gown. Minerva yawned and went to bed. I changed quickly and walked to the couch that Minerva had prepared for me. Blankets and soft pillows covered it and made it look extremely inviting.

I was about to snuggle into the warm blankets, but I heard Emma crying. She was lying on her couch and turned away from me. I sat on the floor beside the couch and asked, "Are you ok, Emma?"

She slowly turned around. Her eyes were red and puffy. She whispered, "Helena."

"I'm sorry," I patted her shoulder sympathetically. "Do you want to talk about her? You might feel better."

She sat up, "Before we were banned from Sentory Public School, all my non-Jewish friends didn't want to be around me. Their parents didn't want them around me either, like I was some sort of disease. I had sat by myself at lunch until Helena came along. We had never talked before, and we soon became good friends. She was so different. She thought and acted differently than me. I think that's how we clicked well. When we had switched to King United, she didn't switch schools. She had stayed home with her mother and didn't go to school. I didn't see her again. I'll never forget her."

I hugged her, "I'm sure she didn't forget you too."

She smiled and lied down, "I feel better now, Jenna."

I walked back to my couch and lied down, "Goodnight, Emma."

She said softly, "I remember Mother had said goodnight to you, me, Anne, and Papa every night in the barracks. She had missed you so much. Even though she drove me crazy, I really miss her."

I pulled the blankets over me and said softly to myself, "I miss her too."

Chapter Twenty-Five

Cecil woke us up early. He shouted, "Wake up, girls! I have great news!"

I groaned and sat up from the couch. It reminded me of when I had slept on Heidi's couch. Cecil was dancing around the room just like Heidi had done. I asked, "What is it, Cecil?"

He said excitedly, "I got two tickets! I got the last two tickets for the train leaving this morning to Switzerland!"

Minerva walked in wearing a robe, "Cecil, dearest, why were you out so late?"

"I wasn't out late. After I had bought the tickets, I had come in and everyone was asleep. I wasn't very tired, so I went downstairs and checked on inventory in the restaurant."

"What a good man," she stood on her tiptoes. He quickly squatted so she could kiss him. "I think I'll keep you."

"Quickly get dressed, girls!" Cecil said. "The train leaves in about an hour!"

We quickly changed clothes in the bathroom. Emma wore a purple long-sleeved dress, a warm hat, grey tights, a jacket, and boots. I wore the same, but my dress was green. We came out of the bathroom. Cecil had moved our bags by the door. Emma said graciously, "Thank you so much for helping us. I really wish there was some way we could repay your kindness."

We both hugged Minerva and Cecil. Minerva smiled, "Oh, you're welcome, girls."

"Anything for a friend," Cecil added. "Let's head out to the car."

He packed our bags into his small car, and we piled inside the car. He started the car and drove down the road. I stared out the window most of the time. I noticed the streets were clearer. Not many people were outside this early in the morning. It was eerily quiet.

We finally arrived at the train station. It didn't take very long to get here. Cecil pulled into a parking spot. I noticed Emma was asleep. I shook her awake. She sat up quickly and looked around. Her eyes were wide and scared, "Is this it? Are we at the train station?"

Cecil nodded, "Yes. I'll grab the bags."

"What's wrong?" I asked. "Did you have a nightmare?"

"Don't you recognize this place?" she asked quietly. I looked at the train station. It seemed familiar to me, but I wasn't sure. "It's where we lost Papa."

The realization hit me like a brick to the head. A train pulled into the station. I imagined soldiers pushing people into crowded cars. I imagined soldiers carrying Papa away and Mother crying for him.

Cecil opened the car door for me, and I stepped out of the car. The cold air made the hair on my arms stand up straight. We tried to take our bags from Cecil, but he insisted on carrying them.

We walked together to the station, and Cecil and Minerva walked behind us carrying our bags. We stood together and waited to board the train. Cecil set the bags down, "Here are your papers and tickets. Hand both of them to the conductor. He'll hand you your papers back."

We both nodded. I turned around to face the train. This time it will take me to a new life instead of death. Minerva said softly, "Don't be scared, girls."

I turned to face her, "I've lost most of my family, friends, and life. I've battled the cold. I've been beaten and abused by many people. I've been experimented on by cruel people. I've seen things 16 year olds should never have seen. I don't know fear."

Emma squeezed my hand and nodded, "We're ready."

Cecil hugged us tightly, "I hope you both have a good, merry life. Stay safe, girls."

"Thank you so much, Cecil," I whispered in his ear. "Thank you a thousand times."

"You're welcome a million times," he replied.

"All aboard for Bern, Switzerland!" cried the conductor. People handed their papers and tickets to him and boarded the train.

"I think you're ready to board, girls," Minerva smiled. Cecil let go of us.

We quickly hugged Minerva. Emma said, "Thank you for the clothes, Minerva."

"You're welcome. Take care of each other," she said softly.

We handed the conductor our tickets and papers. He read them, handed the papers back to us, and stepped aside to let us on the train. We turned and waved goodbye to Cecil and Minerva, and they waved back. We boarded the train and our future.

We were escorted to our rooms. Emma and I shared a bunk bed. There were four bunk beds per room. Two people across from us slept in the same bunk. Two others slept in the bottom bunk. They were a family; they didn't want to be separated.

I know the feeling.

Two couples used the other two bunk beds. All of us kept to ourselves. The only person that talked to everyone was a little girl that belonged to the family.

I sat on my bottom bunk. I was thinking about Mallory, and the girl plopped next to me and started talking, "Hi, my name is Maggie! My full name is Magdalene Jean McKinney, but I like Maggie better. What's your name?"

"Maggie, don't bother her!" scolded the mom. "I'm sorry, miss."

I smiled weakly, "It's fine. My name is Jenna."

Maggie smiled, "I like that name!" She is missing her right canine. She said. "I lost my tooth last night! The tooth fairy hasn't come yet though!"

The mom looked down sadly. The father patted her back sympathetically. They talked quietly, and the mother looked like she was about to cry. I guess the tooth fairy was broke.

"When do you think she'll come, Mommy?" she asked. I choked a little. When she said "Mommy" it reminded me of when Mallory talked about her "Mommy."

Her mom wiped her eyes and replied, "Soon, love, soon."

The little girl walked to her mom and sat in her lap. Her mom played with her long, red hair. It reminded me of when my mother would play with my hair.

I climbed to the top bunk and sat next to Emma. She was biting her nails. She hasn't done that since she was 8 years old. She looked at me and sighed, "In the car, I had dreamed of what happened to Mallory. When I saw what they were doing to her, it reminded me of Anne."

"Yeah, me too," I agreed. I saw Anne's face instead of Mallory's. I almost heard the cries of my mother too. "I can't believe she didn't make it. We were so close."

Emma shook her head, "It was my fault. I should've carried her longer. She wouldn't have fallen down."

I patted her shoulder, "No, it's my fault. I had set her down to talk to the old man. I should've picked her up again."

Emma smiled weakly, "I guess we can't really beat each other up on this. If I had carried her, I would've ran slower, and they would've caught me. The same goes for you."

I nodded, "Yeah, but I still wish I would've done something. She didn't deserve to die."

"No one deserves to die, Jenna." Emma pointed out. "There wasn't anything any of us could do. If we had tried to help, they would've beaten us too. I'm just glad I still have you."

"Did you see all the people watching? It was like we were their entertainment for the day," I said, shuddering uncomfortably. I announced. "Gather around folks, watch the daily Jew slaughter!"

She punched me, "Jenna, don't say that."

I looked down in shame. We were silent. I closed my eyes and leaned against Emma. She rubbed my back and hummed softly. I had never thought I'd get to be with my sister again. All the times I had taken for granted to hang out with her. She's the only family I have now.

When I had first gotten into that truck that fateful night, I didn't know this was where I'd eventually end up; on a train to Switzerland with Emma, the last member of my family. I didn't know I'd lose so many friends and family members, or become a test subject for inhumane experiments, or fall in love, or beaten to a pulp, and then beaten some more. I didn't know I'd actually hate being skinny, or lose all my hair, or the feeling in my legs.

I felt hot tears slide down my cheeks. Emma gently brushed them away, "Jenna, it's ok." She hugged me tightly. "We're away from all that now. No one can hurt us anymore."

After dinner, Emma and I sat in the coach car. We watched the snow-capped mountains fly by us. The landscape was very beautiful. I've never been anywhere close to the mountains.

We discussed what we would do in Switzerland. I told her about my plans to be a journalist in a newspaper. She smiled, "You'd be a great journalist, Jenna."

"What will you do?" I asked.

She gripped the armrest, "I don't want to sell my body ever again, but what if we can't make it?"

I took her hand, "Then we'll starve. I don't want you to do something like that either."

She smiled weakly, "I don't want you to do that either. It was terrifying."

We were silent for a moment. She said softly, "I remember one girl accidently got pregnant. She was like me; having sex in exchange for more food. I heard they did horrible tests to women who were pregnant. The thought of me possibly becoming pregnant was terrifying."

I looked at her in shock. She nodded, "One day, she had started throwing up everywhere. Everyone had thought she was sick, but I knew the truth." Tears moved down her cheeks. "She was only 14 years old, Jenna. Her name was Penelope, and she was Polish. Soon, the soldiers found out she was pregnant and sent her to the hospital. I never saw her again." Emma and I sat in silence. Shortly after that, we went to bed, but didn't sleep.

Many days passed, and we were almost to Bern. Emma and I were excited and exhausted. There wasn't much to do on the train, so we usually stayed in our little cabins. We only left the cabin to eat, and then we'd sit in the coach car and talk for a little bit. Emma and I definitely had cabin fever. We couldn't wait to stretch out on land.

One night, Emma decided to go to bed early. I sat in the coach car alone. I thought about Bern. Many people live there, and I hope Emma and I will be able to find an apartment to share, or a job.

I was worried about my dream job. It's a big risk. I'm not sure if they'd let a 16 year old girl into the newspaper business. However, on my papers it says I'm 17 years old. Would they even believe that?

What if Emma and I can't even find a job? What if there aren't any apartments available at all? I shivered at that thought. Living on the streets terrified me. I'd already seen street life in the ghettos in Amsterdam. Diseased people crawled around in the street and begged for food or water. I wonder if Bern and Amsterdam are around the same size? I guess I'll find out.

I watched the sun setting behind a mountain. I sighed, maybe this was a bad idea. How are we going to make it in Bern? We're just two, teenage girls on our own and barely any money between us.

The train moved around a curve of a mountain. As we traveled the side of the mountain, I saw the sunlight glisten off the majestic Alps. It made the mountain glitter with unimaginable colors. The sight filled me with hope.

This was a different kind of hope. It wasn't an "I hope I survive the night," hope or "I hope I'll get a meal today," hope. This hope made me believe I could make it in this city. This hope gave me the strength to know I will survive, I will live, and I will make all of my family proud. I'm living for myself and them now. I won't just make it in this city, I will thrive in this city.

This isn't the end of the road, it's the beginning.

ABOUT THE AUTHOR

Veronica Fuxa is 16 years old. She had trouble with verbal communication skills when she was younger, and as a result is a very visual learner. Reading and writing became very easy and comforting to her. She started writing stories when she was about 11 years old. This is her first published book. She lives in Enid, Oklahoma with her parents and brother.

Veronica loves to hear from her readers!
To send her a message, or learn more information about her,
visit her website at

www.veronicafuxa.com
And like her on Facebook!
www.facebook.com/authorveronicafuxa

Made in the USA
Las Vegas, NV
10 December 2020